DEATH
Treads the Boards

LESLEY COOKMAN

Published by Accent Press Ltd 2019

Accent Press Ltd
Octavo House
West Bute Street
Cardiff
CF10 5LJ

ISBN 9781786152817
eISBN 9781786152824

CHAPTER ONE

'So you see, I thought she might make a good – um – *addition* to your company.' Mrs Jeremy Coutts smiled nervously across the desk at Dorinda Alexander.

'Oh, go on, Dolly.' Ivy, Lady Anderson, seated next to her friend, leant forward across the desk and poked Dorinda on the arm. 'You took in that Velda, and Amy here, when they was – *were* – both in trouble.'

'And look where that got everybody,' said Dorinda. 'I really don't want to go bringing trouble down on the house any more. I've had three lots of trouble in my life already and it sounds as though this – Jessie, is it? – is more of the same.'

'Jessie Jones,' confirmed Mrs Coutts - formerly Amelia, Lady Washington, alias Amy West, Music Hall performer.

'You've heard of her, Dolly, 'course you have.' Ivy gave Dorinda another poke. 'Doing well, she is. Smaller halls, mainly, but she's popular.'

Dorinda sighed and looked out of the window at the slope up to Victoria Place. The sun was shining, and as yet few holidaymakers graced the promenade. It was barely the beginning of the season, and The Alexandria Concert Hall hadn't yet opened. In fact, the company - or concert party, as they were still being called - hadn't been finalised, so Ivy and Amy's request was not quite so impossible as she hoped

1

it was. She turned back to her petitioners.

'If she joins us she will be expected to be part of the ensemble. It won't be all solo spots. She might not be prepared to do that.'

'Oh, she is!' Amy assured her quickly.

'You've told her all about it, have you?' Dorinda gave her a mocking smile. 'And I suppose she's sitting in a carriage just out of sight?'

Ivy and Amy looked at one another guiltily and Dorinda, who hadn't really thought this was the case, started. 'Oh, she isn't! You don't mean it!'

'Well, we thought you'd want to see her,' said Amy. 'You did me.'

Dorinda subsided into her chair, shaking her head. 'Ivy, was this your idea?'

'No, it was mine,' said Amy. 'And, er, Maude's.'

'Maude?' Dorinda fairly shrieked. '*Maude*?'

Ivy was on her feet. 'Calm down, Dolly. She ain't done nothing wrong.' Ivy's accent had a tendency to slip under stress.

The office door opened and Maude Beddowes hovered in the opening. Plump, comfortable-looking and at the moment red-faced with embarrassment, she was Dorinda's right-hand woman in the company and married to Will, the former leader of the concert party.

Dorinda passed a weary hand over her brow, hiding a smile.

'Come on, traitor,' she said. 'Tell me all.'

'Oh, I'm sorry, Dolly.' Maude hurried in and hovered beside the desk. 'Will and I saw her in London when we was up doing that series of smokers last winter.'

The smokers were private events at which concert party performers could earn money during the off-season.

'Good, isn't she?' Amy turned enthusiastically to Maude. Her accent tended not to slip quite as much as Ivy's, although they both came from the same East End of London background.

'Very good. We 'aven't seen Vesta Tilley, but we was told she was as good as 'er.' Maude peered into Dorinda's face, anxious eyebrows raised.

'Vesta's something special,' said Dorinda, who *had* seen the exceptional lady in question. She stood up. 'Very well, then. Bring her in, Maude. I take it you actually told her about us?'

'No, Miss.' Maude shook her head vigorously. 'It was Amy – Mrs Coutts – 'ere. And Ivy backed 'er up.'

'Since when have you called me "Miss"?' asked Dorinda. 'You must be worried! Oh, go on, go and fetch the lady.'

All three women watched Maude hurry up the slope and turn left, and out of sight at the top.

'Tell me again why she wants to come here?' Dorinda sat down again.

'Well.' Amy sighed. 'It's her pa, see. He belongs to one of those chapel groups.'

'Methodists?' suggested Dorinda.

'I don't know.' Amy shook her head.

'They don't 'old with drink,' said Ivy, with a sniff. 'Or anything on the stage.'

'Temperance Movement?'

3

'Dunno,' said Ivy. 'I don't reckon there's that many o' them, but they started linin' up outside the last couple of Halls Jessie was playin', and in the end she got the sack. Oh, you know: "We don't like to lose you, but…" And she don't want to go back to dashin' between the grubby little supper rooms like they used to.'

'Is she underage?' Dorinda was even more wary now.

'Gawd luv you!' said Ivy. 'She's nineteen! She's been doin' this for three or four years now. See it isn't 'er real pa – it's 'er step-pa. 'E married 'er ma after Jessie went off to London. Welsh, 'e is.'

'Ah.' Dorinda was aware of the strong Chapel movement in Wales. A chapel on every corner, some said, and militant with it. She could imagine how well a male impersonator from the Music Halls would go down with them.

'And this is her, is it?'

Maude was coming back down the slope, accompanied, a little reluctantly it seemed, by a slight young woman in a plain grey jacket and skirt with a small straw boater on her head.

'That's 'er.' Ivy peered through the window. 'Not much to look at, is she?' She grinned at Dorinda. 'But you wait!'

They heard the main doors open, and after a quick knock on the office door, Maude appeared, triumphant.

'Miss Jessie Jones, Miss, er, Dolly.'

The small grey person followed Maude into the room. Dorinda stood up and held out a hand.

'Miss Jones,' she said with a smile. 'And you know Lady Anderson and Mrs Coutts, of course.'

Jessie Jones gave her a nervous smile and briefly shook hands.

'Well, sit down.' Maude had fetched an extra chair from the foyer and shoved it against the back of Jessie Jones' legs. She sat down abruptly.

'I hear you'd like to work for us?'

'Er – yes.' The voice, like the person, was small.

'And you realise it's mainly ensemble work interspersed with solo spots? You'd be prepared for that?'

'Oh, yes.'

Dorinda regarded her, head to one side. Jessie began to fidget.

'I'm a little worried,' said Dorinda after a moment, 'about your reasons for wanting to come here.'

Jessie's mouth dropped open, and after a shocked gasp, Amy and Ivy broke into simultaneous protestations. Dorinda turned to them in some amusement.

'I know what you've told me, ladies, but now I want to hear Jessie tell me herself. This would be a very different life she'd be living.'

Jessie directed panicky eyes at Maude, who frowned at Dorinda.

'She's only a kid, Dolly.'

'And I'm not her mother,' said Dorinda abruptly. 'Neither are you, Maude. Jessie has to stand up for herself. I'm sure she had to do that on the halls in London, didn't you, Jessie?'

'Er, yes.' Now Jessie wouldn't meet Dorinda's eyes.

Dorinda let out an impatient exclamation. 'Ivy, Amy – are you sure about this?'

Ivy and Amy exchanged glances.

'Well, we thought so,' said Ivy.

Dorinda stared out of the window for a moment.

'So what is it, then, Jessie? What are you not telling me?' She turned sharply towards the girl, silencing the others with a raised hand. After another moment's silence she spoke again, less sharply.

'Jessie, you must see that I can't take you on if there's any doubt about your motives or your honesty.'

'We told you, Dolly,' Ivy interrupted. 'It's her dad. Step-dad.'

'Is that all it is, Jessie?' asked Dorinda, watching Jessie's face go white. She seemed to crumple before her eyes, and Maude hastily stepped forward. Dorinda's eyes narrowed.

'Ivy, Amy – could you leave us for a minute?' She smiled at the two women, who looked indignant, but did as she asked. Maude moved up to sit alongside Jessie and took her hand.

'Do you know what the trouble is, Maudie?' Dorinda kept her eyes on Jessie's face.

'I guessed a bit of it.' Maude cleared her throat. 'You have, too, ain't you?'

Dorinda nodded, then said gently: 'He attacked you, didn't he, Jessie?'

The white face turned bright red.

'Where was this?'

Jessie had difficulty speaking, but eventually managed. 'On me way home.'

'More than once?' asked Dorinda.

Jessie nodded.

'Just because of what you were doing for a living?'

'He said…' Jessie swallowed. 'He said…'

'She didn't deserve no better,' put in Maude.

'So it wasn't simply a beating?' said Dorinda.

Maude shook her head.

'Ah.' Dorinda looked down at her desk, then stood up and went to the door. Outside, Amy and Ivy stood looking anxious.

'Come in, ladies.' Dorinda held the door open for them and they both hurried forward to Jessie.

'Well now, all we've got to decide is whether Jessie keeps her name or we change it.' Dorinda smiled as four faces looked up hopefully.

'She can stay then?' said Ivy.

'Oh, I think so. But we've got to think of the circumstances, and we don't want any more of the company being put at risk, do we? So what we've got to weigh up is whether Jessie's name is well enough known to be a draw, or well enough known to bring her step-father down here.'

'She was getting quite well known,' offered Maude.

'We had this same situation with me, didn't we?' mused Amy. 'People do find you.'

Jessie sat up straight, assuming a determined expression. 'I'll change me name.'

'Are you sure?' said Maude. 'Seems a pity.'

'What's yer middle name?' asked Ivy suddenly. ''Ave yer got one?' In her excitement, Ivy's accent had slipped disastrously.

'Matilda!' said Jessie, looking surprised.

Ivy and Dorinda looked at each other and beamed.

'Jessie Matilda!' they said together.

'But won't her pa recognise that? He'd know her middle name,' said Amy.

'No, 'e don't.' Jessie shook her head. 'Took no notice of me or me brothers and we'd all gone by the time 'e moved in.'

Dorinda took a deep breath. 'That's it, then. We'll take a chance. Now, Jessie, would you like to show me what you can do?'

She led the way into the empty auditorium and up to the stage. Amy and Ivy sat down in the front row, while Maude urged Jessie up the steps to the stage and stepped back. Dorinda sat down at the piano and waited.

Jessie came nervously towards her.

'It won't be the same without me clothes,' she said.

'I know.' Dorinda smiled. 'I won't bite. Can I play something for you?'

'I got me own songs. I could do one without music?'

Raising an eyebrow, Dorinda nodded. 'Do you want a note?'

Jessie's face broke suddenly into a broad smile. 'That white one right in the middle!' she said.

Dorinda grinned in return and struck middle C.

And before their eyes, Jessie became a street urchin. Completely without self-consciousness, she strutted and tumbled about the stage until she finally came to a halt leaning on the proscenium arch.

'Bravo!' called Dorinda as she, Ivy, Amy, and Maude broke into spontaneous applause.

Flushed and smiling, Jessie came back down the steps. 'Was I all right?'

'You certainly were!' Dorinda patted her shoulder. 'You won't mind being a girl for the ensemble numbers, will you?'

'No, I done that in London. 'Ow many in the company?'

'At the moment, three men, Will, Ted and Algy, and four girls, Betty, Phoebe, Patsy and Maisie.'

'I tell you what, Dolly,' broke in Amy. 'I could teach her a couple of the numbers, couldn't I? See, Jessie,' she turned to the younger woman, 'I come down last season -' Dorinda noticed that Mrs Amelia Coutts was slipping into the former Amy West, 'to hide, exactly like you, so I learnt all the routines.'

'We might not use all the same ones, Amy,' warned Dorinda.

'Well, you got to keep The Fairies!' said Amy.

The Fairies, a routine first seen on the London stage, had been adapted by The Alexandrians, being improved by a new member of the company and further improved by Amy. It had been a great favourite of the audiences last season.

'Oh, yes, The Fairies!' chorused Ivy and Maude.

'Is that the Gaiety one?' asked Jessie.

'Based on that, yes,' said Dorinda. 'You know it, then?'

'Not to say I seen it,' said Jessie, 'but I've 'eard of it.'

'Good.' Dorinda nodded. 'And now – have you got digs yet?'

Amy opened her mouth, but shut it again as Dorinda glared at her.

'No.' Jessie looked worried.

'I daresay the girls will be able to sort you out, eh, Maude?' Dorinda made a face at Maude, who nodded. 'Are you going back to London tonight?'

'She's coming 'ome – home – with me,' said Ivy. 'I'll bring 'er down when you want 'er.'

'I'll let you know when we've sorted out her digs,' said Dorinda. 'I'm sure Jessie won't mind sharing with a couple of the other girls, will you?' She turned and smiled at Jessie.

'You ring me up,' said Ivy, who was inordinately proud of being the owner of a telephone. As she and Sir Frederick had also caused one to be installed at The Alexandria, this was a not unreasonable suggestion.

'So, Maudie,' said Dorinda when Ivy, Amy and Jessie had gone, 'tell me the rest of the story.'

Maude looked surprised. 'Rest?'

'How did you find her? Or how did Amy find her? She didn't just pop up out of nowhere, did she?'

Maude sat down on the other side of the desk and stared at her steepled fingers for a moment.

'Well,' she began, 'we come across her when we were doing the smokers, as I said. And then Ada – you remember Ada?'

'Ivy's sister? Of course.'

'Well, she come to see us. She says there's this girl who looks like she's going to get the sack and what about bringing her down here? She remembers Velda, and then Amy.'

Dorinda sighed heavily. 'Yes, you said. What happened next?'

'So Will and me went to see her – Jessie, I mean – and

10

sort of suggested it, but she said she wasn't going to run away.' Maude looked up, straight into Dorinda's eyes. 'So then when we met Amy – took us to tea at a posh 'otel, she did – we told her about it. And – well, you know Amy.'

'So Amy went to see her and convinced her to come down here.' Dorinda scowled at her friend.

'No, no, Dolly! You've got it wrong. Jessie still didn't want to come down. See she hadn't been sacked then. But then her pa starts up these – I don't know what to call them…'

'Protests?' suggested Dorinda.

'Yes, them, and making a fuss, so the owners of the halls just says enough's enough, sort of thing. And then, although we didn't know that till after, he attacks her.'

'And then she came to you?'

'No.' Maude shook her head. 'She went to Ada. So Ada took her in for a few nights and telephoned Ivy.' Ivy and Sir Frederick had a telephone installed for Ada as well, although she kept it quiet in her own neighbourhood. 'And Ivy telephoned Amy. And there we are.'

Dorinda sat for a moment in thought. 'And when her stepfather attacked her – it wasn't just an ordinary attack, was it?'

'No.' Maude's face glowed red. 'Disgustin' old… Practically his own flesh and blood.'

'Yes.' Dorinda shivered. Maude was instant contrition.

'Oh, Dolly – I never thought!'

Dorinda looked up and tried a smile. 'Oh, come on! At least I had the protection of Sir Frederick and Ivy, not to mention all of you. Most girls in my position would have been left on the streets. And at least Jessie isn't expecting a child.' Dorinda glanced quickly at Maude. 'She isn't, is she?'

Maude shook her head. 'I think we'd have known by now.'

'All right.' Dorinda nodded again. 'And now Aramantha's gone to try her luck in London, we've got room to fit her in without too much trouble. Betsy and Maisie could fit her in at their lodgings, couldn't they?'

'At least they won't be as much trouble as Aramantha would have been,' said Maude with a sigh.

CHAPTER TWO

Three weeks on and Jessie Matilda had fitted in very well, as Dorinda had predicted. Her seemingly mouse-like persona came alive on stage, but she was quiet enough off stage for Betsy and Maisie to positively mother her. She shared their lodgings, made no trouble, and altered her own Silver Serenaders pierrot costume. Amy had donated hers, but being a little more statuesque than Jessie, a certain amount of taking in and taking up was necessary. Jessie's routines, The Urchin, The Respectable Tramp, The Man-about-Town, and The Soldier were all diverse, allowing Dorinda to feature different combinations as she changed her programme twice a week.

Already, people were coming especially to see Jessie, and often coming back two or three times a week. The company, unlike many, were generous, and accepted Jessie's talent and revelled in the fact that it reflected on them all a certain amount of distinction.

'If it goes on like this,' said Maude one morning during the fourth week, 'we'll have to add another row of seats by July.'

'And a gallery by next year,' said Dorinda thoughtfully.

'A what?' Maude looked startled.

'A gallery. Balcony – call it what you like. And if we fitted proper theatre seats – you know, in a curve – we'd get a lot more people in.'

Maude looked at her with her mouth open. 'A proper theatre, then?'

'Of course. Then we could hold concerts during the off-season – even pantomime, perhaps.'

'Oh, come on, Dolly! There's no visitors in the winter! That's why we all go up to London.'

'I didn't, this time,' said Dorinda.

'Well, you taught piano, didn't you? Still don't see how you made enough to keep the wolf from the door.' Maude shook her head.

'I played for the Mayor's Christmas Ball and a few other occasions,' said Dorinda. 'And Ivy and Sir Freddie's Christmas Entertainment.'

'I'm surprised anyone went to that,' said Maude. 'I thought they was out of favour with the gentry.'

'Oh,' said Dorinda, gazing out of the office window at the slope up to Victoria Place, 'you'd be surprised what a bit of notoriety can do. People were only too eager to come along. I think they all wanted to go home and gossip about how dreadful it all was – instead, they all had a perfectly pleasant evening attended by the Honourable Jeremy and Mrs Coutts and the Earl of Hawkesley. Not to mention a few other lords and ladies.' Dorinda grinned. 'We all rubbed our hands with glee.' Her tone changed as her gaze sharpened. 'Maudie – do you know who that is?'

'Who's what?' Maude turned to follow Dorinda's gaze. 'Where?'

'Up on Victoria Place. Standing against the railings – not facing the sea.'

14

'I dunno.' Maude squinted. 'Just someone waiting for someone? Why?'

'Because I've seen him every day this week. If he was here at night, I'd say he was waiting for one of the girls, but he's only been there in the afternoons.'

Maude looked worried. 'You don't think..?'

'Anything to do with Jessie?' supplied Dorinda. 'Well if he is, he's not making trouble – yet. We'll just keep an eye on him. Perhaps ask Will, or Ted and Algy, to get him in conversation.'

But by the time Ted and Algy had strolled up the slope to start a conversation with the loiterer, he had disappeared. And it wasn't until the Friday evening that he reappeared - this time with a half a dozen others, mainly women, who arranged themselves across the top of the slope, denying access to The Alexandria.

'Whatever do they think they're doing?' Dorinda gasped, as Maude pointed them out. By this time, Dorinda was in her silver pierrot costume and an angry crowd of would-be audience members were trying to force their way down. However, as the women blocking their way appeared to be respectable, there had so far been no manhandling.

'Maudie – telephone to Deal and ask them to send Constable Fowler here.' Dorinda whirled out of the office, threw open the front doors and ran up the slope.

'What is going on here?' she panted as she got to the top.

Two of the women forming the human barricade turned to face her. The first, tiny, wearing large spectacles and a superior expression, drew herself up to her maximum height, which must have been all of four feet ten inches, and glared at Dorinda. The second, taller and slightly drooping, with a red nose and watery eyes, tried to avoid looking at anyone.

'We are preventing the deluded public from viewing this disgusting spectacle,' squeaked the smaller of the two. Dorinda had to stop herself from laughing.

'I see,' she said mildly, and turned to the crowd now staring interestedly at this confrontation. 'Did you come here to see a disgusting spectacle?' she asked.

There was laughter, a chorus of "Noes" and a few "Yeses". She turned back to the two women, aware that the rest of their supporters had melted away.

'I think you had better move away, don't you?' she said pleasantly. 'A policeman will be here shortly, and after all, I don't believe you are suffragists, ready to suffer jail for your cause?'

The shorter woman gasped in outrage.

'Disgusting women!' she squeaked. 'As bad as your – your – your *harlots*!' She went bright pink as she uttered this word, and her taller friend shut her eyes and moaned quietly.

Out of the corner of her eye she saw the burly frame of Constable Fred Fowler moving along Victoria Place, followed, surprisingly, by a younger man, also in the uniform of a constable, with a fresh face and a neat dark moustache.

'Tell me why you are here, then,' prompted Dorinda. 'Who brought you?'

'It's against the teachings,' whispered the Tall One. 'Brother Anarawd told us.'

16

'The teachings?' said Dorinda.

'Now, now!' broke in the comfortable voice of Constable Fowler. 'What's all this then?'

'We were doing our duty!' gasped the Short One.

'Oh? And what duty was that?' asked Constable Fowler. He took her arm, nodded to his fellow constable, who took the arm of the Tall One, and began to move away. 'Don't you worry, Miss Dolly,' he said over his shoulder. 'We'll see to it.'

Dorinda watched, puzzled, with her hands on her hips, as the two women were led away. There was no sign of the rest of the protesters. She smiled at the crowd.

'Come along in then,' she said. 'Don't worry about them.'

'But,' said a voice in her ear, as she moved back down the slope amid the crowd of would-be audience, 'they was doin' that in London. We saw them, didn't we, Bert?' said Mary.

'Blocking theatre entrances?' asked Dorinda.

'Yes.' Bert spoke in the other ear. 'Said they didn't 'old with theatricals, same as Mary said, and especially women dressin' up as men.'

'Said it was against the Bible,' said Mary.

'They didn't sound Welsh,' mused Dorinda.

'Welsh?' Mary sounded surprised. 'They don't make no trouble, do they? Not like the Irish.'

'Shhh!' Bert darted round behind Dorinda and grabbed Mary's arm. 'Never know who might be listenin'!'

Dorinda pondered this cryptic remark as she retreated to her office, leaving Maude to deal with the tickets. Was this

Brother Anarawd Jessie's stepfather?

During the interval in the afternoon's show, Dorinda went back into the space behind the stage the company proudly called the "dressing rooms", intending to bring the conversation round to the disturbance earlier in the afternoon. She didn't have to.

'Was that my stepfather out there?' asked Jessie the moment Dorinda appeared. The rest of the room went silent.

'It was mainly two women,' said Dorinda. 'There were a few others with them, but by the time I got there they'd gone. Melted into the crowd.' She went over to Jessie and made her sit down. 'Now,' she said quietly, 'why did you think that?'

'Because that's what they used to do,' said Jessie. 'Try and stop people from coming in. What did they say?' She fiddled with the edge of the pink draperies the girls wore for The Fairies, the item which closed the first half.

'What's your stepfather's name?' asked Dorinda.

'Michael Evans.' Jessie looked nervous.

'Then it wasn't him.' Dorinda felt as much relief as Jessie obviously did. 'They mentioned someone called Brother Anarawd.'

Jessie's whole body sagged, and she smiled up at Dorinda. 'Oh, thank you, Miss Dolly.' She looked round at the other girls. 'It wasn't him!' she said, and they all crowded round happily, patting her on the back and kissing her cheek.

'All the same,' said Dorinda later to Maude. 'It's a terrible coincidence, isn't it, that we heard that the stepfather was a militant Welsh churchman, and one turns up soon after Jessie starts performing here.'

'Do you think it's him, then?' Maude was pulling on her hat, preparing to go out for between shows sustenance.

'I don't know.' Dorinda leant back in her chair, shaking out her hair. 'I hope Constable Fowler comes to tell us what those women said.'

It wasn't until the interval in the evening show that Maude bustled round to ask Dorinda to come out to the office. The faces she was making told Dorinda that the news was not for the ears of the company, so reluctantly, Dorinda followed her through the auditorium and out into the foyer.

'What is it, Maude?' she asked.

'Police!' whispered back Maude dramatically, and threw open the office door.

Inside, standing self-consciously by the desk, his helmet clasped to his chest, stood the young constable Dorinda had seen in the afternoon.

'Constable?' she said in surprise. 'What can I do for you?'

'Just come to report, Ma'am – I mean, Miss,' said the constable, going rather red in the face. 'Dad sent me... I mean – Constable Fowler.'

'Dad?' Dorinda beamed. 'So you're Constable Fowler, too?'

'Constable Robert, Miss. Dad's Constable Fred.' Constable Robert shifted his feet. 'He said to tell you -'

'Oh, do sit down, Robert.' Dorinda sat down in her chair behind the desk.

'Oh – I – er...' Constable Robert looked round nervously, and finally perched on the very edge of a visitor's chair. 'Dad said... about those women... I mean, ladies...'

'The two who were trying to block the slope?'

'Yes, Miss. He said they was from London.'

'Yes.' Dorinda frowned. 'Two people in the crowd said that, too. And that they were against us on religious grounds.'

'Yes, Miss. They said there was more people there, too, and someone was an -' Constable Robert screwed up his face, 'an abom – abom...'

'Abomination?' suggested Dorinda, hiding a grin.

'That's right, Miss.' Constable Robert gave her a relieved smile. 'Against the Bible, they said.' He frowned. 'They wouldn't say no more.'

'Hmm.' Dorinda frowned down at her hands. 'They didn't say we'd be struck down, or anything like that?'

Constable Robert was obviously shocked. 'Oh, no, Miss! Nothing like that.'

'So that was all?' Dorinda was now tapping her fingers on the desk. 'What did your father do with them?'

'Well, nothing, Miss. He told them they were causing a public nuisance and he said if they did it again, he'd take 'em in charge.'

'I bet he wouldn't, though,' said Dorinda, with another grin. 'So, have they gone back to London?'

'I don't know, Miss. Dad said to tell you we'd be keeping our eye out.'

Dorinda stood up. 'Well, thank you, Constable Robert. It was good of you to come and tell me, and we'll keep an eye out, too.'

She watched as the young man walked quickly up the slope, now with his helmet jammed on his head, unhooked his bicycle from the railings and rode swiftly off.

'Fred Fowler's son,' she told Maude as she went to go back through the auditorium. 'I'll tell you later.'

After the final number of the evening, Dorinda went back into the dressing rooms.

'I wanted to tell you,' she said, sitting down on a wicker trunk, 'that Constable Fowler has told the ladies who tried to block off the slope this afternoon to keep away and go back to London.'

'Who was they?' asked Betty.

'Constable Fowler didn't say, but they were religious, apparently.'

'Did they...' Jessie looked round at the girls. 'Were they...'

'They didn't appear to have anything to do with your stepfather,' said Dorinda, and tried to smile reassuringly. 'Constable Fowler says he and his son are going to keep an eye on them if they don't go back to London.'

'His son?' said Patsy.

'Yes. He was with him this afternoon. He's a constable, too.'

Phoebe, Patsy, Betty, and Maisie all began asking questions, but Jessie merely retired behind the screen and began to change into her outdoor clothes. Dorinda made a face at the other girls, and Betty, assuming an air of importance, nodded and brightly changed the subject.

Dorinda went back to her office through the now empty auditorium and found Maude locking the front doors. While herself changing from her silver pierrot costume into her plain grey flannel skirt and white blouse, she told Maude what Constable Robert had said.

'I still think it's suspicious, Maude,' she said, struggling to roll her hair up into a semblance of respectability. Maude took over.

'Fred Fowler didn't say anything about a man, though,' she said.

'But there was a man with them – at least one,' said Dorinda. 'And there was that one I saw leaning up against the railings. I pointed him out to you – I'd seen him for a few days. He was there with that group at first, but he'd disappeared by the time I got to them.'

'Don't you think you're just looking for trouble? After all that bother last year with Amy, and before that with Velda?'

'But Amy and Ivy admitted that was why they thought Jessie would be safe here.' Dorinda sighed. 'I've become a home for displaced performers.'

CHAPTER THREE

There was no repeat of the unpleasantness during the next week, no sightings of lone men loitering at the top of the slope and Dorinda began to relax. Jessie was becoming more popular than ever, and although Dorinda expected a certain amount of resentment about this from the rest of the company, it never materialised. What did materialise, however, was far more unexpected.

It was Saturday afternoon, with no performance until the evening. Dorinda had decided that as it was change-over day for the holidaymakers, it was better that the company went to the station to both meet and see off their changing audiences. It paid off in two ways: those leaving were left with an indelible memory of The Alexandrians wedded to that of Nethergate, and would be keen to return next year, while newcomers would be introduced to the company and possibly persuaded to attend at least one performance. Sometimes it could be awkward, as when a returning member of the public claimed undying friendship with a member of the company and expected to be remembered – sometimes intimately. But this Saturday, someone arrived and found no one to meet her.

Dorinda was sitting at her desk sighing over the accounts when a flurried movement on the slope outside caught her eye. The next moment there was a hammering on the door, after which she heard raised voices and the office door burst open.

'Dolly!' gasped Maude but was pushed aside.

''Ere, Miss, you got to take me back!'

Dorinda gaped. On the other side of the desk stood Aramantha Giles, nee Ethel Small, now arrayed in what she obviously thought was the latest fashion and in a state of considerable agitation.

Dorinda looked helplessly at Maude, who looked helplessly back and spread her hands in a gesture of hopelessness.

'Aramantha,' said Dorinda. 'Sit down, do, and tell me what's the matter.' She went around the desk, pausing in front of Maude just long enough to whisper 'Tea', and urged the girl into the best visitor's chair.

'Now,' she said. 'Tell me what's wrong.'

'Well,' gulped Aramantha, 'I got to leave me job.'

Dorinda's eyebrows rose. 'Job? What job?'

If Aramantha had been a horse, she would have shown the whites of her eyes. As it was, she visibly shied.

'Come on, Aramantha,' urged Dorinda, taking hold of the girl's shoulders. 'What job?'

'I bin doin' chorus,' whispered Aramantha.

'Well, that's marvellous! Where?' Dorinda sat back, smiling.

Aramantha sat, opening and closing her mouth for all the world like a fish, thought Dorinda, her frightened eyes fixed on Dorinda.

'Well, it can't be the Gaiety anymore, can it? In London?'

Aramantha heaved a great sigh, dropped her gaze, and nodded.

'Come on, then. Tell me all about it.'

'I couldn't get no work, see.' The girl shifted uncomfortably on her chair. 'I kep' bumpin' into this same girl in all the places I looked for work, an' in the end, she said I could go alonga her that night.'

Maude came in silently and put a tea tray down on the desk.

'So you went?' prompted Dorinda.

Aramantha nodded.

'And it wasn't what you were used to?'

Aramantha shook her head.

Dorinda looked up and exchanged worried glances with Maude.

'What did they want you to do, ducks?' asked Maude, perching on the desk.

There was a pause, then… 'Take me clothes off,' mumbled Aramantha.

Dorinda swallowed a horrified exclamation.

Maude patted the girl's hand. 'Yes, I've seen some o' those,' she said, and looked sideways at Dorinda. 'So did they give you a job?'

'I couldn't get no work,' whispered Aramantha. 'I 'ad to do it.'

''Course you did,' said Maude. 'How long have you been there?'

'Coupla months.'

'And why have you got to leave?'

Aramantha's head dropped even lower and she suddenly

burst into tears.

'Never mind about that now,' said Dorinda hastily. 'Here, have your tea.'

She placed a cup and saucer on the desk in front of the sobbing girl, then got up and left the office. Maude was better equipped to deal with this situation than she was.

She walked through the auditorium and the dressing rooms to the back door, which led out onto the little gallery that ran around The Alexandria, overlooking the beach. From here the brightly painted bathing machines could be seen, drawn up at the water's edge. Families crowded round Marvello's Punch and Judy tent, and up on Victoria Place sat in deckchairs or leant against the railings. Dorinda viewed all of this with none of her usual complacency, worried about the scene she had left behind. Presently, the door opened, and Maude slipped out to join her.

'I got Will to walk her back to ours,' she said. 'She can stay in the sitting room tonight, until we decide what to do with her.'

Dorinda felt her heart sink. 'We?'

Maude looked at her in surprise. 'Well, she hasn't got anyone else, has she?'

'Look, Maudie,' said Dorinda, with a firmness she didn't feel. 'She chose to leave us "for something better" she said, didn't she? It isn't our job to pick up the pieces when she failed to find it. And we don't exactly owe her anything, after the business with Velda. She was lucky we let her stay.'

Maude set her lips firmly. 'I know that, Dolly. And I'm no more sympathetic than what you are, but when I said I'd

seen some of those, I meant it.' She looked down on a small family eating a picnic on the beach below. 'Happy, they look, don't they? Hard to believe that kiddie there could turn into an Aramantha. But she could.'

'Come on, Maudie. What places? Don't try and change the subject.'

Maude heaved a sigh and turned around, her back to the beach. 'Will and I got taken to a couple when we was up last winter.' She shook her head. 'Supposed to be proper old-fashioned music halls, but they weren't. Dreadful places. Back rooms behind pubs, couple in the Arches, some in respectable-looking houses. All got up with a stage of sorts, and tables and chairs for the customers. Only they was all men.'

'Ah,' said Dorinda, 'I begin to see. Was she expected to do anything except sing and dance – or wasn't she even supposed to do that?'

'Oh, yes. They had routines, if you could call 'em that. But if one of the customers picked her out, she was supposed to... oblige.'

' That's disgraceful!' gasped Dorinda.

Maude looked at her kindly. 'For all you're such a good business lady, you're awful innocent, Dolly!'

Dorinda felt her cheeks becoming hot. 'I know things -' She took a deep breath. 'Go on, Maudie. I just...'

Maude patted her arm. 'I know, Dolly. Comes from a sheltered background.'

They fell silent. Eventually, Dorinda turned and faced Maude. 'Have we got room for her?'

'In the show, you mean?' Maude looked doubtful. 'She

could join the chorus, but there's no room for solo spots.'

Dorinda sighed. 'And she won't like that, knowing our Aramantha.'

'If she wants us to take her in, she'd have to put up with it,' said Maude.

'I thought you wanted us to take her in?'

'Yes, but more to protect her, if you know what I mean.'

'But from what?' asked Dorinda, swinging round to look at the sea again.

Maude frowned. 'I don't know.'

'We'll talk to her tonight,' said Dorinda. 'No sense in worrying about it now.'

However, during the interval in the evening performance, Maude appeared in the dressing room looking harassed.

'It's Aramantha,' she whispered in Dorinda's ear. 'She turned up banging on the door to be let in. What could I do?'

'Wretched girl!' hissed Dorinda. 'Where is she now?'

'Sitting in the back row of the auditorium. Sniffing and shaking her head. You know what she's like.'

'Do you want me to have a word with her?'

'No.' Maude stood upright, firming her lips. 'I shall tell her to keep quiet, or out she goes. Is that all right?'

Dorinda grinned. 'Perfectly, Maudie.'

When she resumed her seat at the piano, after acknowledging the audience's appreciation with a bow, she allowed her gaze to sweep lazily over the back rows, where she finally picked out Aramantha, looking slightly cowed, with a rather militant Maude standing behind her. Satisfied,

she struck up the opening number for the second half.

At the end of the show, she made her way out to the foyer, exchanging goodnights with the last members of the audience. Maude, showing them out, jerked her head in the direction of the office. Dorinda went in.

'What are you doing, Ethel?' she said sharply.

Aramantha, her hand in the desk drawer, started back so fast she fell against the back wall.

'N-nothing, Dolly! I mean – Miss,' she gasped.

'Then come, sit here and show me your hands and pockets,' said Dorinda, placing a visitor's chair in front of the desk.

'Ain't got no pockets,' mumbled Aramantha.

'Take off your jacket,' ordered Dorinda.

Colouring a deep red, Aramantha awkwardly shrugged off her jacket. Dorinda heard Maude bolt the outer doors and called her in.

'Search her, Maude.'

'S-search..?'

'She had her hand in the desk drawer when I came in,' said Dorinda. 'If that's how she intends to treat us when we're offering her sanctuary, I think we should tell her to go.'

Aramantha's face crumpled. 'I weren't…' she began on a sob.

'Weren't what?' asked Maude. She looked through the jacket and shook it out. 'Nothing here, Dolly.'

Dorinda softened her voice. 'All right, Aramantha. What *were* you doing? And while you're telling us that, you can tell us why you're down here and what scared you.'

CHAPTER FOUR

Maude pulled over the other visitor's chair, Dorinda took her own seat and they both looked at Aramantha, who looked back nervously from one to the other.

'I thought I could come back,' she said eventually, in a shaky voice.

'You left us,' said Dorinda. 'We had to replace you.'

'With that Jessie Jones!' Aramantha's face showed a spark of animation.

'She's Jessie Matilda now,' said Maude. 'Do you know her?'

'I only know she got the sack 'cause of 'er pa.'

Dorinda narrowed her eyes. 'And how do you know that if you don't work at a proper hall?'

'Word gets 'round.' Aramantha hung her head.

'And do you know her pa?' asked Maude.

'Course not!' said Aramantha quickly.

Yes, you do, thought Dorinda. Now, how, I wonder? She changed the subject.

'Why did you want to come back? Yes, I know all about the sort of hall you were playing, and what you were expected to do, but you stuck it out for a couple of months, didn't you?' She glanced quickly at Maude. 'And I don't like to bring it up, but there was the business with Velda and the gentlemen, wasn't there?'

Aramantha held her gaze, but her eyes filled with tears and her lip trembled.

'So come on, Aramantha. Why were you frightened?'

'I was followed,' the girl whispered eventually. 'This bloke – dunno 'oo 'e was – was waitin' outside. 'E started whisperin' about sin and 'ow 'e could save me. An' then one night – two nights ago, it was – 'e grabbed me, an' -' She broke off, her face contorting. 'Dis*gus*tin' it was.' She shuddered. 'An' I got up, an' all I could see was 'is 'ands – …' She stopped and buried her face in her hands.

After a moment, Maude put her arm round the girl's shoulders and said quietly, 'Did he hurt you bad?'

Aramantha shook her head, taking her hands away from her face. 'No – that was all I saw… 'e couldn't – couldn't – oh, it was dis*gus*tin' I tell you. An' then 'is bloody 'ands...'

'And you didn't tell anybody?'

'No. Next mornin' I just slung me things in a bag and come down 'ere.' She looked up at Dorinda. 'I'm sorry.'

Dorinda smiled at her. 'Never mind. Now, if you don't mind sharing lodgings with the other girls, we could fit you into the chorus, but as you saw tonight, we've no room for any more solo spots.'

Aramantha opened her mouth, caught Dorinda's eye, and closed it again. She nodded.

'Right.' Dorinda stood up. 'Now I'm going to get changed. You can wait in the foyer for us.'

'Not on me own!' Aramantha looked panicked.

'I'll come with you,' said Maude. 'You'll have to manage your own hair, Dolly!'

Dorinda saw them out into the foyer, went behind the

screen in the corner and slipped out of her silver pierrot costume. She just hoped Maude could rustle up a costume for Aramantha, not to mention something for the evening dress sections. It didn't look as if the girl had brought anything with her.

'Didn't think it through,' Dorinda muttered to herself through a mouthful of pins, as she tried to put her hair up.

Finally ready, she went out into the foyer and found Maude and Aramantha surrounded by the rest of the company. Aramantha, she noted, was looking a lot happier and even rather smug.

'Come along then, everyone, time to go home.' Dorinda turned to Ted and Algy. 'Will you see the girls back between you? Will has charge of Maude, me, and Aramantha.'

The little group separated and turned to face her.

'Is Aramantha coming back, Miss – Dolly?' asked Betty.

Dorinda smiled. 'Maybe. Now come along, we need to lock up.'

'But – but what about Jessie, Dolly?' asked little Patsy nervously.

'What about her?' Dorinda smiled down at Jessie, who was clutching Patsy's arm. 'She's doing very well.'

A little sigh of relief went up, which told Dorinda clearly how much more her company liked their newest recruit than they had liked Aramantha, whose expression had gone from smug to petulant.

Finally, Dorinda got them all out of the building and locked the front doors. She watched as Ted and Algy carefully herded their charges up the slope, keeping Jessie

firmly between the two of them, although it didn't appear that there was any great need for protection tonight.

'What's goin' on?' asked Aramantha, as Will walked his party up behind them. 'You got problems again? It's that Jessie, ain't it?'

'We've had problems with a few religious fanatics,' said Dorinda dismissively.

'Oh, them!' scoffed Aramantha. 'Don't like no drinkin' or enjoyin' yerself, do they?'

Maude looked across at her curiously. 'Didn't they ever bother you where you was working?'

There was a slight pause before Aramantha turned her head away, mumbling: 'Couldn't get in, could they?'

Maude and Dorinda exchanged glances. As they reached the top of the slope, Dorinda was aware of Aramantha's eyes darting swiftly from left to right, as she tried to tuck herself in between Will and Maude.

'Something's wrong,' she murmured to Maude.

When they arrived at their shared lodgings, Dorinda showed Aramantha into the small sitting room the landlady had set aside for their use.

'You'll have to sleep in here tonight,' she said, 'but we'll see if we can't find you something better tomorrow. Now, perhaps Maude would make us a cup of tea while you tell us exactly what you're afraid of, and who you think might have followed you down here.'

Aramantha gaped. Dorinda's lips twitched.

Maude, hastily turning a chuckle into a cough, took the kettle to fill it up in the kitchen before coming back to set it on the little spirit stove beside the fire. She found

Aramantha perched miserably on the very edge of one of the upright chairs, and Dorinda comfortably relaxed on the couch. Will had disappeared into the bedroom.

'Come on, then, girl,' she said, standing, arms akimbo, in front of Aramantha. 'Tell Miss Dolly.'

'Ain't nothin' -' began Aramantha..

'To tell?' suggested Dorinda. 'Or to do with us? Come, now. Neither of those things are true, are they?'

Aramantha slowly shook her head.

'What is it?' asked Maude sharply.

Aramantha sighed and finally sat back on her chair. 'Them Baptists – or whatever they are.'

'So you *did* have trouble with them?' said Maude.

'The men used to come in. The women never.'

'They used to stand outside? With banners?' said Dorinda.

'Only in the daytime. Nighttimes the men come in.'

And you were scared they might be down here? You were nervous coming back here, weren't you?'

'You said you'd had trouble,' began Aramantha.

'Just with some women trying to prevent people from going down the slope,' said Dorinda. 'No men.' She wasn't going to mention Jessie's unsavoury stepfather yet.

Aramantha nodded, watching as Maude poured boiling water into the big brown teapot. 'And no other trouble?'

'No,' said Maude, while Dorinda shook her head. 'You were here last year – that was the most trouble we had.' Aramantha had the grace to colour slightly, acknowledging her own part in the previous year's problems.

Maude poured tea and handed out cups. 'I'll go and find

blankets in a minute,' she said. 'You'll be all right here?'

Aramantha nodded again, then looked at Dorinda. 'That policeman still comin' down here?'

'Policeman?' Dorinda looked blank. 'Oh – Constable Fowler? His son's been round after the religious women bothered us. He's a constable, too.'

'No.' Aramantha looked sly. 'You know. That one from London. The one 'oo fancied you.'

'Inspector Colyer?' put in Maude, diverting Aramantha's attention from Dorinda's suddenly pink face. 'No, we haven't seen him. Nothing for him to investigate, is there?'

Aramantha dropped her eyes. 'No,' she mumbled, and Dorinda raised her eyebrows at Maude.

'Come on then, Maudie' she said. 'I'm going to bed and you can fetch Aramantha some blankets.' She patted Aramantha's shoulder. 'Goodnight.'

Outside on the landing she whispered, 'There's more to this than meets the eye. What do you think we should do?'

'Keep an eye.' Maude shrugged. 'Nothing much we *can* do, now you've said we'll take her in.'

'Oh, I thought it would end up my fault.' Dorinda grimaced. 'I can't help feeling, *here we go again.*'

CHAPTER FIVE

With a certain amount of difficulty, Dorinda fitted Aramantha back into the company, although in a less prominent position. Luckily, the former ensemble member had kept her old Silver Serenaders costume and had the sense to bring it, together with two evening dresses, down to Nethergate with her after all. Although not altogether pleased at her reduced status and inclined to be dismissive of Jessie, she caused less of a problem than Dorinda had feared, and for a few days the company appeared to be working as normal. Until, that is, Dorinda, Maude and Will arrived at the top of the slope from Victoria Place to find a banner strung right across it, tied to the railings.

I will set no wicked thing before mine eyes Psalm 101.3

After standing horrified and silent for a long moment, Dorinda and Will both lunged forward to tear the banner down.

''Ere!' shouted a voice. 'Wot you doin'?'

Dorinda swung round in time to see a red-faced Constable Fowler Senior approaching on a wobbly bicycle.

'Fred!' shouted back Will. 'It's us! Come and look.'

Constable Fowler dismounted clumsily, propped his cycle against the railings, took off his helmet and mopped his perspiring forehead.

'Sorry, Miss,' he gasped as he came up to them.

'Couldn't see it was you.'

'Look at this, Fred,' said Will. 'Those women again, I reckon.'

Constable Fowler peered at the banner and frowned.

'I ain't seen 'em since, Will,' he said. 'Reckon they come back?'

'Somebody has,' said Dorinda.

'And done this,' said Maude. 'Calling us vile things. I mean!'

'Give us a hand with this, Fred.' Will was wrestling with the string at one end of the banner. 'Get the other end.'

When the banner had been removed, Constable Fowler solemnly folded it up and put it in the little satchel behind his saddle. 'Evidence,' he said seriously.

'I don't suppose you'll catch who did it,' said Dorinda. 'Not unless you catch them red-handed.'

'No, Miss.' Constable Fowler shook his head mournfully.

Dorinda was thoughtful as she, Maude and Will finally made it down the slope and into The Alexandria.

'What's up, Dolly?' asked Maude as she and Dorinda went into the office while Will went off through the auditorium. 'It doesn't look as if they've done any damage.'

'No.' Dorinda sat down behind the desk and gazed out of the window.

'What, then?' Maude sat down on one of the visitors' chairs. 'You're not happy about something.'

Dorinda transferred her gaze to her friend. 'Do you think it was those women?'

'The banner? Looks like it.' Maude turned and peered up

the slope. 'But where are they?'

'They were warned off by the police. It makes sense that they should come round after dark.' Dorinda shook her head. 'But somehow it doesn't ring true.'

'Why? Who else would do it? And use Bible words?'

'Aramantha's scared of something, although she seems better now. Do you think…'

'Nobody would have bothered to follow that silly girl down here,' said Maude. 'She's not worth it.'

Dorinda was amused. 'She wouldn't like that! But no, I agree. Then you could say the same about Jessie – why would anyone bother? But she's genuinely afraid of her step-father.'

'Well, it isn't Aramantha's step-father, is it? You leave it to Fred Fowler.' Maude stood up.

By this time, the rest of the company had begun to arrive, and Dorinda went through to the dressing room behind the stage to tell them what had happened.

Aramantha snorted. 'Tryin' to scare us? What do they reckon they can do?'

Everyone looked at her in surprise. She went rather pink. 'Well, those women, weren't it?'

'You weren't there though,' said Dorinda. 'What do you know about it?'

'You said,' Aramantha reverted to the mumble she'd seemed to have adopted.

'Yes, I did mention it,' said Dorinda, looking around at the rest of the company. 'Did you say anything, girls?'

'Might've done,' said Maisie, looking confused. The others looked equally bewildered.

'Well, don't worry about it.' Dorinda turned to go. 'Constable Fowler has it in hand.'

'Which one?' asked Betty. 'The old one, or the young one?'

There were appreciative giggles from the other girls and, smiling, Dorinda left them to explain to the obviously inquisitive Aramantha.

Interesting, though. Aramantha had made a lucky guess about the women who had targeted The Alexandria. Based, perhaps, on incidents experienced in London? Had this anything to do with her precipitate departure? Dorinda frowned as she crossed the auditorium. She just hoped nothing else would happen. Last season had been bad enough – she had hoped this one would be calm and trouble-free.

The day wore on. The afternoon performance went smoothly, more packed than usual due to a lowering sky outside that promised a downpour, a promise fulfilled just as the audience was leaving.

'If it doesn't stop soon there'll be no one in this evening,' said Maude, peering out of the office window at the hurrying crowds.

'It can't be helped, Maudie,' said Dorinda philosophically. 'At least we had more people in this afternoon.'

'Want me to go out and get a pie?' Maude turned from the window. 'I'll take the umbrella.'

'I don't like sending you out in this,' said Dorinda.

'Don't be silly!' said Maude cheerfully. 'Come on, hand it over.'

Dorinda handed over some money, Maude collected the umbrella from the stand in the corner by the door and left. Dorinda watched her scurrying up the slope to Victoria Place. Twenty minutes later, she was back.

'That was quick!' Dorinda looked up from the desk in surprise.

'There weren't anybody there,' said Maude, obviously puzzled. 'Fat Aggie said she'd heard that someone was holding some sort of meeting over on the jetty. P'raps they've all gone there?'

'Meeting? I wonder what sort of meeting?' Dorinda opened the greasy paper parcel and picked up her pie. 'Not the Suffragists?'

'Fat Aggie didn't know.' Maude stood the umbrella back in the stand, where it dripped disconsolately into the tray at the bottom. "I'd better take Will his pie.'

Dorinda sat pondering about the meeting at the other end of town while eating her pie. Suffragists, End of The World prophets, political reformists – she sat up straight. And religious crusaders.

'Well, if it is them, people won't stay long in this weather,' remarked Will, when he and Maude came back to the office.

'No, they'd rather come in here in the warm,' said Maude. 'Now don't worry, Dolly. Just you think about what new numbers we're going to put into the show next week.'

Dorinda gave her friend a weak smile and cast a quick glance at the pile of bills sitting on the corner of the desk, which included payments for songs. She sighed. Audiences rarely realised that performers had to pay to perform the popular songs the public wanted to hear.

'All right, I'll be good.' She grinned at the two others and began sorting through a pile of song sheets.

The rain stopped just in time for the evening performance, and the auditorium was filled with a steaming horde of holidaymakers. Water dripped from hats and umbrellas formed puddles round feet on the floor, but the audience didn't mind. They were there to enjoy themselves.

And enjoy themselves they did. Damp though the audience was, it did nothing to dampen Dorinda's spirits, even when she noticed Constable Fowler Junior standing at the back of the auditorium towards the end of the second half.

'Constable Robert wants a word,' Maude whispered as Dorinda left her seat at the piano to go through to the dressing room area. She paused, shrugged her shoulders, and sighed.

'Come on, then.' Maude led the way through the auditorium through patrons, all of whom wanted to congratulate Dorinda, though none realised that she was the owner of not only the company, but the building too. Eventually they reached the foyer, where Constable Robert stood stiff and very much ill at ease by the office door. Dorinda opened it with a friendly smile and preceded him inside.

'Now, Constable,' she said, taking her seat behind the desk. 'Do sit down.'

'I'd rather stand, Miss,' said Constable Robert, clasping his helmet in front of him.

Dorinda felt the first trickle of alarm.

'What is it?' she asked.

Constable Robert's cheeks became suffused with red. 'It's them religious coves, Miss!' he burst out. 'It's one o' them!'

'Who is? What is?'

'Been murdered, Miss! Up beside the Cliff Terrace steps.'

CHAPTER SIX

Dorinda sat transfixed. Becoming aware that she was staring at Constable Robert with her mouth hanging open, she found her voice.

'Oh, not again!'

Constable Robert shot her a startled look.

Dorinda shook her head to clear it and stood up. 'I'm sorry, Constable, but your father knows how much trouble we've had here with -'

'Yes, miss!' Constable Robert broke in hastily. 'I know. He's here now, up at the steps, so he sent me to tell you.'

Dorinda's brows drew together. 'So he thinks it's something to do with us again, does he?'

'Well, no, Miss, but seeing as how those old – those ladies seemed against you last week, and then with that banner...'

'Ah, I see.' Dorinda frowned down at her desk. 'But how does Constable Fowler know the man is one of the – er – religious lot?'

'There was men in the crowd, Miss,' said Constable Robert reprovingly. 'And this one was seen in the area on his own, too.'

Dorinda's mind flew back to the lone loiterer she had noticed on several afternoons before the advent of the Short One and the Tall One. Yes, there had been at least one man among their supporters, and she remembered wondering then if it had been Jessie's stepfather.

'Do they – do you – know when he was killed?'

Constable Robert frowned. 'No, Miss. He was found earlier. I expect Dad – Constable Fred will ask around.'

There were a hundred questions Dorinda wanted to ask, but she realised Constable Robert wouldn't be able to answer them.

'Well,' she said at last, 'at least it couldn't have been one of us – we were all in here.'

'No, Miss – I mean, yes, Miss.' Constable Robert's fluctuating complexion returned to red again.

'So why did Constable Fowler want you to tell us?'

Constable Robert's brows drew together. 'Like I said, Miss, because you'd had trouble...'

'Yes, I see.' Dorinda gave him a tremulous smile. 'Well, go back and tell him we'll do anything to help. Not that I can think of anything we *can* do...'

When the young constable had gone, Dorinda called Maude into the office.

'But it's got nothing to do with us!' said Maude when Dorinda had told her what had happened. 'Why tell us?'

Dorinda repeated what Constable Robert had said. 'I can see why Constable Fowler thought we'd like to know, but as I said, we were all in here, so it can't have anything to do with us.'

''Course it hasn't.' Maude drew herself up self righteously. 'I'll go and tell the others, shall I?'

Dorinda sighed. 'I suppose you'd better. Warn them to keep away from Cliff Steps when they go home - and then could you come back and help me with my hair?'

However, when Dorinda had changed and Maude had bundled her hair into its usual state of semi-respectability, they found the entire company waiting for them in the foyer.

'What's the matter?' asked Dorinda.

They all shuffled their feet looking furtive. Eventually Will said, 'Jessie and Aramantha are worried.'

Dorinda shot a glance towards Maude. 'About the banner and the protesters?'

'Yes, Miss – Dolly.' Betty stepped forward, her arm protectively around Jessie. 'Could it be like a – a warning?'

'A warning? To us?' said Dorinda in surprise. 'How could it be?'

Betty, and indeed all the others, looked confused. Aramantha, Dorinda noticed, was trying to make herself inconspicuous at the back. She sighed and tried again.

'Look, whatever's happened, it isn't anything to do with any of us. As I said to Maude and Constable Robert, we were all here all evening, weren't we?'

Neither Jessie nor Aramantha looked convinced by this, but the rest of the company appeared reassured. Dorinda, Will, and Maude saw them all out of the building and up the slope. As they followed after locking up, they could see the glow of lanterns gathered around the bottom of Cliff Steps. Dorinda shuddered and looked away.

'What's the betting we'll have another visit from the police in the morning?' said Will gloomily, as they turned up the high street on their way home. 'It's just not fair.'

When Dorinda arrived the following morning to unlock

and found Constable Fred Fowler waiting for her, she was inclined to agree that it wasn't, indeed, fair. Constable Fred seemed only too aware of her feelings and shifted from one foot to another miserably.

'Well, Constable?' asked Dorinda with a sigh, as she led the way into her office. 'What is it now?'

'This body, Miss. The one -'

'You found last night, yes Constable. What about it?'

'It's been identified, Miss.'

'Yes?' prompted Dorinda, when the constable appeared to dry up. 'Identified as whom?'

'That Brother Anarawd them women – ladies – were talking about. Their leader, like.'

'Oh.' Dorinda sat down behind the desk, feeling that she had known this all along. ' What has that to do with us?'

'Well, Miss,' began Constable Fred, going almost purple in the face, 'seein' as how they was against you – the concert party, like – we, well, the inspector thought...'

'We might have got rid of him?' Dorinda was conscious of anger and fear in equal parts. 'How ridiculous!'

'Yes, Miss, I know.' The constable leant forward confidingly. 'But he don't know you.'

'Is this the inspector from Deal?'

'Yes, Miss. See, the woman who said who it was – the body, I mean – she was one of those women... you know?'

'I know, Fred. Which one? The short one?'

'Yes, Miss. Well, she carried on something awful about you – the company, I mean.'

'I see.' Dorinda nodded. 'Accused us of being abominations before the Lord, I suppose?'

'I don't know about that, Miss...'

'Oh, I do.' Dorinda sighed again. 'All right, Fred. What do we do now?'

'I think I'm supposed to ask everyone questions,' said Constable Fred, looking anxious.

Dorinda smiled. 'All right, then. As I'm the only one here, you can start with me.'

'Er – yes, Miss.' Fred looked doubtful. 'I think the inspector wanted to know where you were last night -' he held up a hand, 'I know, Miss – I already told him, you was here. And so was all the others. And then he wanted to know if you – any of you - knew the, um... body before.'

'Before?' Dorinda wrinkled her brow.

'Before now, Miss. I mean, was he *known* to anyone.'

'Goodness, I don't know! And neither will they unless they know who it is you've found. None of us have seen him, have we?'

'No, Miss.' Constable Fowler looked puzzled. 'Do you think you should all go and have a look at him? Don't seem right, somehow.'

'I don't think I would like that,' said Dorinda. 'Nor would the other ladies. Why don't you ask the inspector what we should do? Is he here?'

Constable Fowler looked embarrassed. 'No, Miss. He's still in Deal.'

'So you're in charge are you, Fred? That's a little unfair, don't you think?'

Now Constable Fowler looked confused again, and heaved a deep sigh.

'Why don't you telephone him, Fred? We've got a

telephone -' she waved at the instrument, 'and so has he. Then you can ask him for further instructions.'

The constable looked dubious. 'I don't know, Miss.'

'Why haven't you got a telephone yet?' Dorinda asked, genuinely curious. 'It must be very difficult when you have to take orders from someone in Deal.'

Constable Fowler looked wistfully at the instrument on the desk. 'It is, Miss.'

'I'll leave you to make the call in private.' Dorinda hesitated, wondering if it would be tactful to ask him if he knew how to operate the telephone.

'Thank you, Miss.' Constable Fowler gave her a timid smile and reached towards the instrument. Dorinda left the office and closed the door.

As she did so, the front door opened and Betty, Maisie, Phoebe, Patsy and Jessie entered in a rush.

'No Aramantha?' asked Dorinda.

Betty, as usual the spokesperson for the girls, shook her head. 'Still asleep, Dolly. At least, that's what she wanted us to think.'

Phoebe gave a disparaging sniff. Dorinda eyed her shrewdly. 'Didn't believe her, Phoebe?'

Phoebe gave an embarrassed little laugh. 'Sorry, Miss – I mean, Dolly. No, I didn't.'

'Phoebe shares with her,' explained Patsy. 'No one else wanted to.'

'Oh, dear,' said Dorinda with a sigh. 'She isn't causing trouble, is she?'

'Not really,' said Betty. 'Just a – I dunno, a sort of…' She looked round helplessly at the other girls.

'Atmosphere,' supplied Dorinda, and nodded. 'Yes, I know, and I'm sorry. But what else could I do but let her come back? She had nowhere else to go.'

'And she was scared,' said Jessie.

They all turned to look at her in surprise.

'I know the look,' she said. 'And I could feel it. Even though she don't like me.'

'She doesn't like anybody,' said Maisie.

'But she's been quite well behaved on stage, hasn't she?' asked Dorinda. 'No sly digs that I can't see?'

'She's been all right,' conceded Betty reluctantly. 'Considering she ain't got no solos.'

At this moment, Constable Fowler emerged from the office. The five girls all started back in alarm.

'Did you get through, Constable?' asked Dorinda, holding up a placatory hand to the girls.

'Yes, M – Miss.' The constable took a deep breath. 'Could I have a word?'

Dorinda nodded and stepped through the open office door. 'All right, girls. I'll come and see you in a little while. Will and Maude are backstage.'

Constable Fowler followed her inside and closed the door behind him.

'It seems he was from London, Miss. The body.'

'Oh? How do they know?'

'I'm not sure, Miss, but the inspector asked about anyone who come from London.' He put an enquiring head on one side. 'Two of your young ladies do, don't they?'

Dorinda's stomach seemed to swoop downwards. She nodded.

'That young Jessie? The one who does the sailor and the tramp?' He peered at her shrewdly. 'Didn't I hear tell her dad -'

'Is a militant Baptist, or Methodist or something. Yes,' said Dorinda.

'And your Ara – Arath – that girl? She come from London, too, didn't she?'

'A few years ago, yes,' said Dorinda, wondering where this was going.

'But she's been in London these last few months, Will tells me.'

Inwardly cursing Will, Dorinda nodded again.

'I think the inspector will want to talk to them, Miss.' Constable Fowler sounded apologetic.

She sighed. 'Yes, I'm sure he will.' She sat up straight and squared her shoulders. 'Well, we'll all be here all afternoon and evening, Fred. At your disposal.'

Constable Fowler nodded and turned for the door.

'I'm really sorry, Miss,' he said over his shoulder, and left the room.

Dorinda sat staring out of the office window for a few minutes, in time to see the constable retrieve his bicycle and cycle sedately along Victoria Place towards The Square. She also saw Aramantha Giles emerging warily from Cliff Steps.

CHAPTER SEVEN

Dorinda waited until she saw Aramantha approach the big front doors of The Alexandria, then stepped out of the office into the foyer, where she stood with her arms crossed in front of her, waiting.

Aramantha quietly opened one door a crack and slipped silently inside. Closing it just as quietly, she turned and uttered a high-pitched squeak of surprise.

'Well, Ethel?' said Dorinda deliberately. 'Why were you hiding from Constable Fowler? And what were you doing up at Cliff Steps?'

Aramantha once again gave her an impression of a landed fish.

'Come on, girl!' Dorinda was impatient. 'You knew Constable Fowler would want to talk to you. What do you know about the dead man?'

'Nothing! I don't know 'oo it was, do I?'

'I don't know. You certainly didn't see him last night – you were here, as I can confirm. But did you know he was coming to Nethergate, whoever he was?'

'I dunno!' Aramantha almost wailed. 'Honest! I dunno 'oo it was.'

'But…?'

Aramantha twisted her hands together. 'I seen a bloke the other day.'

'Go on.'

'It was one o' them from – from – er…'

'Where you were working?'

Aramantha nodded.

'One of the regular patrons?' Aramantha looked bewildered. 'I mean, one of the men who came and sat at the tables?'

'No.' The girl stared down at the floor. 'One o' the others,' she mumbled.

'The ones who scared you?'

She nodded.

'And you think it's him?'

Aramantha shrugged.

Dorinda sighed. 'Well, go and join the others at the back. The constable will be back later, I expect. You can tell him then.' She decided to say nothing about the impending visit of the inspector.

Which, she decided later, was just as well, for when she looked up from her piano sometime before the interval in the afternoon performance, she spotted a familiar figure standing at the back of the auditorium leaning nonchalantly against the wall. Aware that her breathing had changed, and her face felt suddenly hot, she took a deep breath and concentrated hard on the keyboard.

As the applause died away for The Fairies, as always, the last item in the first half, she left the piano and hurried through the auditorium and into the foyer.

'Good afternoon, Inspector Colyer,' she said, satisfied that she had taken the London inspector by surprise.

'Miss Alexander.' He gave her a small bow.

'I rather thought I might see you here.' She hadn't, but on thinking about it now, she realised that it had been almost inevitable. Someone thought to be from London was murdered on her doorstep, with a possible link to her company. Inspector Jack Colyer was bound to arrive. She opened the office door and ushered him inside.

'And why did you think you might see me?' he asked, perching, as usual, on the edge of her desk as she took her seat behind it.

'There has been a murder in Nethergate, which our excellent Constable Fowler tells me is linked to London. I have two members of my company recently arrived from London, *ergo* The Alexandria must be linked to the murder.'

Colyer studied the floor. 'Put like that…'

'Well, how else am I to interpret it?'

He looked up and the dark brown eyes gave Dorinda a shock.

'There is slightly more to it than that.'

She rather thought there would be. 'Go on,' she said aloud.

'You're employing a young lady, a male impersonator called Jessie Matilda. Very good, she is.' He raised an eyebrow. 'Almost as good as Jessie Jones in London.'

Dorinda sighed. 'Very well, she's the same girl. You knew that.'

'I did. I also know – or I can surmise – why she came here. In much the same way as Velda Turner did, and Lady Amelia, of course.'

'I have become a refuge for runaway artistes.' Dorinda

gave a tired smile. 'I am only thankful that as of yet no male artistes have arrived.'

'I am sure the same thing happens all over the country,' said Inspector Colyer.

'Then why aren't you off investigating in Bournemouth or Scarborough?'

He laughed. 'I don't choose the destination, Dorinda!'

She looked at him disbelievingly.

'I don't! Do you think I make up the cases in order to come down here and plague you?'

She shook her head slowly. 'I don't know. It feels like it, sometimes.'

'Your Lady Ivy's just as much to blame as I am.' He slid off the desk and moved to look out of the window, giving her an opportunity to study his trim figure encased in brown tweed and his slightly curling short brown hair without being observed herself.

'Why is that?' she asked.

'She gets to hear about these waifs and strays, doesn't she? Often from her sister.'

'Ada? Well, yes, that's true, but beside the point. What is the connection you've discovered this time?'

'One of which I believe you are already aware. The man who was, or purported to be, the leader of the little religious group who appeared to be targeting your company.'

'Ah, yes. The man with the strange name.'

'Brother Anarawd, I believe.' Colyer's lips twitched.

'And you think,' said Dorinda, trying to quell a feeling of inner panic, 'that there is more to their antipathy towards us than meets the eye?'

'Wouldn't you say so, Dorinda?'

Dorinda sighed again. Of course she did.

'And what do you think is the cause of this antipathy?'

'Disapproval of all forms of entertainment, as far as I can tell,' said Dorinda, 'and particularly male impersonators.'

'And you just happen to have one.'

Dorinda stared at him in silence until a knock came timidly at the door. She stood up.

'I'm sorry, I shall have to go. I suppose you'll want to speak to the company?'

'If I could speak to Miss Jones and Miss Small after the performance, that would be appreciated.'

'Of course.' Dorinda inclined her head. 'But *please* don't call her Miss Small.'

To her relief, the inspector remained inconspicuously at the back of the auditorium throughout the second half and disappeared before the final applause. Dorinda went backstage and spoke first to Aramantha.

'Could you get changed and come to the office, Aramantha, please?'

'Why me?'

'Jessie, too. Because you were both working in London recently.'

'It's that murder, ain't it? I've a good mind not to -'

'It's the inspector from London, Aramantha.' Dorinda fixed her with a minatory eye.

Aramantha turned away and began climbing out of her evening dress. Dorinda repeated her request to Jessie, who shrank back, terrified.

'There's nothing to worry about,' said Dorinda, hoping there wasn't. 'I'll be there with you. Come to the office when you're ready.'

Maude met her in the foyer looking worried. 'He's waiting outside,' she said in a low voice, at the same time smiling and nodding to the last few members of the audience who were making their way out of the building. 'It's about the murder, isn't it?'

Dorinda nodded. 'I'll just ask him to come in. Keep an eye out for Aramantha and Jessie – he wants to talk to them both, and I don't want them running off before he's seen them.'

She went outside and around the corner of the building, where Colyer was leaning on the railing overlooking the beach.

'Please come in, Inspector,' she said. 'Jessie and Aramantha are on their way.'

He turned and looked up at the sky. 'Beautiful out here, isn't it?' he said. 'You can actually see the sky here. You can't in London.'

Dorinda did not want to get into a discussion on the beauties of the sky with Jack Colyer, so turned quickly to go back inside. She heard him sigh behind her and clenched her fists.

Jessie was waiting nervously outside the office with Maude.

'I'll go and see that Aramantha is nearly ready,' said Maude.

Dorinda opened the office door and ushered both Jessie and the inspector inside.

'Jessie, this is Inspector Colyer from London,' she said, taking her seat behind the desk. 'Inspector, this is Jessie Jones, or Jessie Matilda, as we now know her.'

'Miss Jones.' Colyer held out his hand and, looking surprised, Jessie took it. 'I believe you were recently working in London?'

Gradually, Dorinda saw Jessie relax, as Colyer took her gently through her last few months in London, until her final flight to Nethergate.

'And you haven't seen your stepfather – or any of your family – since you came down here?'

Jessie looked surprised once more. 'No – why would I?'

'I wondered if your mother or your – brothers, did you say? – had been down to see you.'

'I dunno where they are.' Jessie shook her head. 'We all left 'ome before Ma married 'im.'

'Where does your mother live?'

''Oxton. Well, she did. I dunno, now.'

'You think she might have moved?'

'I said, I dunno. I ain't kept in touch.' She shook her head. 'I wanted to get right away from... 'im.'

'You'd already left your mother's home before she married, you said?'

Jessie nodded.

'But he bothered you?'

Jessie's eyes slid sideways to Dorinda.

'He didn't approve -' Dorinda began.

'Please, Miss Alexander.' Colyer cut her off. 'Let Miss Jones tell me.'

Jessie's colour was mounting. Correctly interpreting this

as embarrassment, Dorinda stood up. 'I'll go and fetch Miss Giles,' she said.

Colyer nodded his approval, and Jessie gave her a tremulous smile.

Outside, she found Aramantha and Maude waiting on one of the benches against the wall.

'What's all this about?' Aramantha burst out. 'I want my pie.'

'Inspector Colyer wants to ask you some questions. I'm afraid I don't know exactly what about,' said Dorinda, realising that actually, she didn't.

'Wish I'd never gone to bloody London,' mumbled Aramantha, slumping back against the wall. Dorinda and Maude exchanged despairing glances, just as the office door opened and a white-faced Jessie was ushered out.

'Would you come in, please, Miss – Giles?' Inspector Colyer stood by the open door, his eyes fixed on Aramantha. As she passed him, he shot a glance at Dorinda. The door closed.

'Well!' said Maude. 'What's it all about? Did he tell you?'

'It's that Brother – Brother – 'im that was with them women…' Jessie trailed to a halt.

'Brother Anarawd.' Dorinda nodded. 'That's who the body is, isn't it?'

Jessie looked up, her face a mask of tragedy. ''E said -' she whispered, and paused. ''E said it was my step-pa.'

CHAPTER EIGHT

Maude gasped. 'How does he know?'

Jessie shook her head. 'I dunno.'

'And he wanted to know if your stepfather had been bothering you in London?' said Dorinda.

Jessie nodded.

'And did you tell him?'

'I couldn't,' whispered Jessie.

'Would you like me to tell him?'

Jessie nodded again.

'Off you go, then,' said Dorinda. 'Go and see if they've left you anything to eat.'

Jessie went slowly to the auditorium doors, hesitated, looked back at Dorinda and Maude, then went through to make her way backstage.

'Shall I go after her?' asked Maude.

'Might be as well,' said Dorinda. 'I'll wait for Aramantha. I wonder if Colyer suspects she had something to do with Brother Anarawd in London.'

'What – he was one of those men who...' Maude broke off, looking shocked.

'Perhaps.' Dorinda shrugged. 'Go on, go and see to young Jessie.'

After a few more minutes, the office door was flung open and Aramantha erupted through it, looking as if she was ready to make a bolt for it. Seeing Dorinda, she came to an abrupt halt.

'Have you finished with her, Inspector?' Dorinda rose to her feet. 'Go on, then, Aramantha. Go back and finish your pie.'

The girl looked as if she didn't know quite what to do, and eventually settled for backstage and her pie. Following her departure, Dorinda let out a breath and went back into her office. Inspector Colyer watched as she took her place once more behind her desk.

'Thank you for leaving me alone with them,' he said.

'I probably shouldn't have done,' said Dorinda, 'but Jessie was obviously not going to say anything with me there. And she wanted me to tell you something.'

'Oh?' The inspector's eyebrows rose.

'You rightly guessed – or found out – that Jessie's stepfather had been bothering her in London.' He nodded. 'There was a group of militant protesters – or Baptists, or something – who regularly paraded outside the theatres… halls… where Jessie was working. This man was one of them. Except that he began waiting for her on her way home.'

The inspector nodded again. 'I guessed as much. And…' He paused, looking vaguely embarrassed.

'I believe so,' said Dorinda, answering the implication. 'She hasn't exactly said as much to me.'

'No.' The inspector stood gazing at the floor and thoughtfully pulling at his lower lip.

'May I ask what Aramantha said?' Dorinda was hesitant.

'You may.' He looked up and smiled wryly. 'It didn't

amount to much. But she knew who he was.'

'I thought she did. She was up at Cliff Steps this morning. She said she thought the dead man was one of those who scared her in London.'

'So she said, but no more than that.'

'It's rather a coincidence that this man should be connected to both Jessie and Aramantha, don't you think?' Dorinda watched him warily.

'Is it?' He looked at her with narrowed eyes. 'Just a little bit too much of a coincidence, perhaps?'

Dorinda gasped. 'What?'

He sighed. 'I can't see the connection yet, I admit, but as you said, The Alexandria appears to have become a refuge, and both these – er – *artistes* were bothered by the same man, to a lesser or greater degree, and ended up here within weeks of one another, as did the victim.' He cocked his head on one side. 'What would you think?'

Dorinda nodded slowly. 'I do see, but surely it's cause and effect. Jessie was brought down here by Mrs Coutts and Lady Ivy, and perhaps Brother Anarawd followed her.'

'And then returned to London to harass Miss Small?'

'Oh, I do wish you'd stop calling her that!' said Dorinda testily.

'It's easier than Aramantha Giles, which you must admit is a mouthful.'

'Call her Miss Giles, then. Just as easy as Miss Small.'

'Miss Small or Miss Giles, I gather she arrived somewhat – shall we say precipitately?'

Dorinda blinked. 'If you mean she arrived in rather a hurry, yes, she did. How did you know?'

Inspector Colyer smiled again. 'I'm afraid I can't tell you that. But you see, it means that this man -'

'Jessie said his name was Michael Evans, not Brother Anarawd. Is it?' interrupted Dorinda.

'As far as we know, it is,' conceded the inspector. 'But whoever he is, he must have been in London immediately before Miss Giles came here.'

'To frighten her down here,' said Dorinda.

'Exactly.' He picked up his bowler from her desk. 'I shall have to speak to them both again, I'm afraid. I take it they're working every day?'

Dorinda nodded. 'Afternoons and evenings.'

'Very well. I shall see you tomorrow morning.' He dipped his head, openedi the door and was gone.

Dorinda sat back and regarded the closed door with raised eyebrows. She was still sitting there staring when Maude put her head round the door.

'What happened?'

Dorinda shook herself and sat up straight. 'Nothing much. He believes the body is Jessie's step-father, so does Jessie and so does Aramantha – although she obviously didn't identify him as Jessie's step-father.'

Maude came in and shut the door. 'How did Aramantha know him, then?'

'As one of the men who frightened her.' Dorinda shook her head. 'Although there's bound to be more to it than that.'

'What have we got to do, then?'

Dorinda gave an unladylike shrug. 'Nothing. Just make sure they're both here tomorrow morning. He said he's coming back.'

Maude sighed. 'Makes you feel like a nursemaid, don't it?'

'Or a governess,' said Dorinda with a smile. 'Still, it will be up to the other girls to make sure that Jessie and Aramantha both arrive here in the morning. Aramantha isn't exactly good at getting here on time.'

'It doesn't seem fair to put it all on the other girls,' said Maude.

'There isn't much we can do.' Dorinda stood up. 'Aramantha would not take kindly to coming back to sleep at our digs, and there isn't room with Betty, Jessie, and Maisie – not that she'd be any better there than with Patsy and Phoebe. We'll just have to hope for the best.'

'Perhaps we shouldn't tell her?' suggested Maude hopefully. 'In case she bolts? She's done it before.'

'Perhaps you're right,' said Dorinda slowly. 'We just won't refer to the murder or the inspector at all. How's that?'

Maude smiled. 'Much the best way.'

The remainder of the afternoon, followed by the evening performance, was uneventful. It was obvious that both Jessie and Aramantha were on edge at first, but as time went on, they both appeared to relax, and said 'Goodnight' cheerfully enough when they left The Alexandria. Dorinda heaved a sigh of relief as she locked the big double doors and followed Maude and Will up the slope to Victoria Place.

It came as no surprise to Dorinda the following morning to see Inspector Colyer leaning, once again, on the railings around The Alexandria when she arrived to open the building. He straightened up with a half-smile as he saw her, removing his bowler.

'Good morning, Dorinda.'

She raised her eyebrows at him.

'I'm sorry – should I have returned to the more formal Miss Alexander?'

Dorinda unlocked the doors. 'Please come in.'

Inside, she opened the office door and turned to face him. 'Perhaps you would like to wait in the foyer for the girls to arrive? I have work to be getting on with, I'm afraid.'

This time it was he who raised his eyebrows, but he meekly sat on one of the foyer chairs and crossed his legs. 'May I speak to the young ladies in your office when they arrive?' he asked.

'Of course.' Dorinda inclined her head and retreated into the office.

Despite having told the inspector she had work to do, she sat behind the desk staring into space until he followed his tap on the office door inside.

'Miss Jones has arrived,' he said. 'May I see her in here?'

Dorinda sighed and stood up. Outside in the foyer, she stopped Jessie with a hand on her arm. 'Have you seen Aramantha this morning? Or Phoebe?'

'No, Miss – Dolly.' Jessie shook her head and followed the inspector.

Dorinda went through the auditorium to find the rest of the cast already assembled either on- or backstage.

'Has anyone seen Aramantha?' she asked. 'Maisie? Have you seen her? Or Phoebe?'

'No, Miss. I saw Phoebe earlier, but I didn't knock for 'er when I come out.'

'Right, thank you.' Dorinda turned and went back to the foyer, wondering whether to go to Phoebe and Maisie's lodgings and ask for Aramantha, even if it did risk scaring her.

But just as she reached the foyer, the main doors were flung back, and Phoebe almost tumbled through them.

'Oh, Miss!' she gasped, clutching Dorinda's arm. 'It's Aramantha, Miss! She's gorn!'

CHAPTER NINE

The foyer was suddenly full of people. Maude, followed by the rest of the company, burst through the doors from the auditorium and the inspector flung open the office door. Dorinda tried to calm Phoebe and sat her down on one of the foyer chairs.

'It's all right Phoebe,' she said. 'Just tell us exactly what happened. You saw her this morning, did you?'

'Yes, Miss.' Phoebe gulped. 'When I woke up, she was standin' in 'er shift by the winder.'

'And then what?' prompted Dorinda, as Phoebe seemed to falter to a halt.

'I got dressed an' went an' 'ad me breakfast. Didn't see the others. When I got back, Aramantha weren't there.'

'And?' put in the inspector. Phoebe looked puzzled.

'What did you do then,' explained Dorinda with a quelling look at the inspector.

'Well, I waited, didn't I? Thought she'd popped to – well, you know. But she didn't come back. So I went an' 'ad a look.' She shook her head. 'She weren't there.'

'Were her clothes there?' asked the inspector.

Dorinda felt as if her heart turned over. If they were…

'I dunno.' Phoebe looked helplessly at Dorinda. 'I didn't think…'

Dorinda patted her hand. 'Of course you didn't.' She

looked at Maude. 'Do you think..?'

'Yes,' said Maude. 'I'll go. Come on, Will. Phoebe, Maisie, Patsy – you come too.'

'What about me?' asked Betty.

'You stay here with Jessie, Betty,' said Dorinda. She looked at the inspector. 'What do you want to do, Inspector? Do you want to go and inspect Miss Giles' room?'

'I think perhaps it would be wise,' he said. 'Mrs Beddowes? Do you mind?'

Dorinda, Maude and Will all looked surprised at this evidence of delicacy on the policeman's part.

'N-no, of course not,' said Maude, glancing hastily at her husband.

'Very well.' The inspector opened the main doors and stood back to allow the others to go past him. 'Don't worry, Miss Alexander.'

Don't worry? thought Dorinda as she closed the doors behind them. What else could she do? She ushered Betty and Jessie through the auditorium to the backstage area and made them sit down.

'Now,' she said, 'neither of you can think of any reason for Aramantha's disappearance?'

They both shook their heads. Jessie was, once more, as white as a sheet.

'She never talked to us, Miss – Dolly,' said Betty. 'Except...' she glanced at Jessie.

'She said - things – to me.' Jessie's voice was a whisper.

'What sort of things?'

'About – about what I did.'

'As a performer?'

'Sort of.' Jessie's hands twisted together.

Now, what's all this? wondered Dorinda. 'As a male impersonator, you mean?'

Jessie nodded.

Betty took a deep breath. 'Not just that,' she said and looked again at Jessie, who nodded. 'She said – well, she said…' Betty swallowed hard, 'that it must be *real*.'

'Real? What – that you really were a *man*?' Dorinda was astounded.

'Not exactly, Miss.' Betty was by now bright red.

The penny dropped. 'That you were a woman but you preferred other women?'

Both girls nodded, looking extremely uncomfortable. Dorinda was aware of being furiously angry with the absent Aramantha but struggled to keep it under control.

'Well, unpleasant though that was, it doesn't seem a reason for her to bolt, does it?'

They shook their heads.

'And did she ever refer to what she did in London?'

'Not really.' Betty looked thoughtful. 'Though she did say things like she knew what the real stuff was like. As if what we was doing was – I dunno – just playin'…'

'Real stuff?' repeated Dorinda. Now she wondered exactly what Aramantha had been doing in those unsavoury establishments. 'I wouldn't worry about it. Knowing Aramantha, she was just trying to make herself look important. It's hardly as if she became a big star in London, is it? She wouldn't have come running down here if she had.' She stood up. 'Now, I'm going to make you some tea, then I'm going back to the office.' She tried a bright smile, which, she feared, failed.

Back behind her desk, she tried to concentrate on the ever-growing pile of bills, but failed at that, as well. What was it about her company? About her? Why did these things keep happening? She stood up and went to the window. Would it have been better if she had let Will take over? After all, most concert parties were run by men. And a man wouldn't allow people to take advantage of him. Dorinda reflected with amusement on Will's reaction if Velda, Amy or Jessie had come to him asking for sanctuary, even though she knew Will to be a kind man.

Just then she saw Will himself, leading his little party, arrive at the top of the slope with Inspector Colyer bringing up the rear. She went out to the foyer to meet them.

'Well?' she said, as soon as Will and Maude entered. They shook their heads, looking worried.

'Oh, Miss!' Phoebe tumbled through the door again. 'All 'er things are gone!'

The inspector came through the doors and nodded.

'All right, everyone,' said Dorinda briskly, 'you all go back to the dressing rooms and make yourselves some tea. I want to talk to the inspector.'

Talking softly among themselves they obeyed her, and Dorinda led the way into the office.

'It seems as though Miss Giles has taken it upon herself to leave.' The inspector perched on the edge of the desk. 'The room had been cleared out, no doubt while Miss Phoebe was at breakfast. Including, sad to say, one or two things that weren't hers to take.'

'What? Things belonging to Phoebe?' Dorinda was

aghast. 'How could she?'

'Knowing her past, are you surprised?'

Dorinda slowly shook her head. 'But you surely don't think she had anything to do with the death of this man?'

'With his death, no, but she knew him.'

Dorinda wrinkled her brow. 'But not as Jessie's stepfather? I suppose there's no doubt it was him?'

'No doubt at all. Aramantha said she didn't know his name but he was identified as both Evans and Brother Anarawd – by different people, of course.'

'Who identified him as Brother Anarawd?'

Colyer smiled. 'One of the women who, I believe, rather annoyed you.'

Dorinda laughed. 'The short one? Oh, no! What a shock for her!'

'I didn't see it myself, but I believe she fainted clean away.'

'I'm not surprised! How did she come to see the body?'

'She went to the police station to report him missing. He had been supposed to organise a public meeting at the other end of the beach and failed to appear.'

'Oh, yes! We heard there was one of those the other day. So he was behind that, was he? I'm surprised he would risk appearing in public when he knew Jessie would recognise him.'

'But he had followed her down here. He must have wanted to see her.'

'Mmm.' Dorinda frowned down at her desk. ' If it's the man I think it was, he took care that we didn't see him. He was loitering up there on Victoria Place for a few days before the first time the women tried to blockade the slope, but he always vanished if it looked as though we'd spotted him, and when we confronted the women he just melted away, though I'm sure I saw him.'

'It's understandable enough that he wanted to see Jessie, and equally understandable that she didn't want to see him,' said Colyer, 'but Aramantha? Why did she run away? Even if it was Evans who attacked her in London – she knew he was dead.'

Dorinda was still frowning. 'Betty and Jessie told me something just now. Aramantha was being unpleasant to Jessie apparently, taunting her about – about being a male impersonator.' She looked away. 'And making certain… implications.'

'Ah. I take it they aren't true?'

'Of course not!' Dorinda was indignant. 'But she also said – well, I didn't really understand it, I'm afraid, and I don't think they did, either – but she said something about having been involved in what she called the *real stuff* in London.'

Colyer was silent for so long Dorinda began to get worried. Eventually he stood up and walked to the window.

'Then I think it's quite possible that she was scared of *us*, not the man who attacked her.'

'Us?'

'The police.' He turned to face her. 'I can't be sure, but it seems to me that she was involved – probably against her will – in something illegal. This death has stirred things up.'

'She could also think someone from up there was after her, to – to silence her!'

'Yes, of course. So, two reasons to be scared.'

'Poor Aramantha.' Dorinda shook her head.

'You think so?'

'You said yourself whatever she was involved with, it was probably against her will.'

Colyer sighed. 'I must go.' He picked up his bowler from the desk.

'Before you go – did you find anything in Aramantha's room?' asked Dorinda.

Colyer raised his eyebrows. 'Of course not. It was cleared out. Except for Miss Phoebe's belongings. Why?'

'I just wondered.' Dorinda gave an unladylike shrug.

After he'd gone, Dorinda stared out of the window deep in thought. What now? It wasn't as if Aramantha had been an important part of the company. Her loss would cause very little disturbance to either the performances or the company itself - but linked, as it was, to Jessie's unfortunate stepfather and possibly – although Dorinda hated to think so – to Jessie herself, raised too many uncomfortable questions.

CHAPTER TEN

Making sure the office door was properly closed and no one was lurking in the foyer, Dorinda reached for the telephone. She was not yet completely comfortable with the instrument, but putting in a call to Sir Frederick and Lady Ivy at Anderson Place was becoming almost a normality.

She wasn't surprised when Sir Frederick answered the call himself. He was too fond of his newest indulgence to let a mere servant do so, although the maids were slightly scared of the instrument, and quite happy to let him. It was simply another example of the somewhat individual way Sir Frederick and his lady ran their establishment.

'Dorinda! My dear – how nice to hear from you. Ivy tells me you've taken in another little stray from the Halls.'

'Well, yes, Sir Frederick. Actually it was about that I wanted to speak to you – or rather, to Lady Ivy.'

'Oh? Can I be of any help?'

'I don't really know, sir. It's all rather complicated.'

'Very well, my dear. Ivy's right here. I'll just pass her the instrument.'

There was a shuffling sound, then Ivy's voice came through.

'What's up, Dolly? It isn't that Jessie, is it? Oh, Lordy! I might have known…'

'No, wait a minute, Ivy. It isn't just Jessie. I don't like to talk about it over the telephone, but…'

'Stop! You on this afternoon? Right then. I'm coming down. No – don't argue. Tell Maudie to save a coupla seats – me and – What? Oh, Freddie wants to come, too. We'll come in the motor car. See you later.'

Well, thought Dorinda, sitting back in her chair, at least she'd got someone on her side apart from the company. Although why she should feel that she needed it she wasn't sure.

When they arrived however, it was clear that whatever she thought, Sir Frederick and Ivy were convinced, for they had even brought Billy the chauffeur and May and Ellen the maids, all of whom were ushered ceremoniously into the auditorium.

She went briefly out to meet them in the interval but waited until after the performance to tell them the whole story. She found them in the office, where Maude had installed them.

'Billy's taken May and Ellen to tea,' Ivy explained. 'They're having a lovely time.'

'I'm sure they are,' said Dorinda with a smile. Nowhere else would the staff be taken out in this way, she was certain.

'Come on then, Dolly. What's been going on? That Jessie's all right, isn't she?'

'She's very good,' put in Sir Frederick.

'She is very good,' said Dorinda with a sigh. 'But it isn't just Jessie.'

She told them the whole story, from her possible sighting of Michael Evans to his death, including the reappearance of Aramantha.

'So Inspector Colyer's been down here again, eh?' said Sir Frederick, leaning his chin on his stick. 'Sound man, I thought.'

'Yes, I'm sure he is,' said Dorinda, 'but he won't tell me about whatever's been going on in London, and I need to know how far Jessie's involved.'

' All she did was run away from her pa!' said Ivy. 'Step-pa.'

Dorinda glanced at Sir Frederick. 'He attacked her, Ivy.'

'Oh.' Ivy peered at her shrewdly. 'In *that* way?'

Dorinda nodded.

'Ah.'

'And he did the same to Miss Giles?' asked Sir Frederick.

'We understand that he tried,' said Dorinda, exquisitely uncomfortable talking about this with Sir Frederick. 'But what I want to know is what Aramantha was talking about when she was – er – taunting Jessie about her performances.' She sent Ivy a pleading look. 'I thought Ada…'

'Might know?' Ivy fixed her eyes on a corner of the ceiling. 'Now, then… how could we find out?'

Dorinda and Sir Frederick exchanged amused glances. This was Ivy in plotting mode.

'You don't want to go up to London again, do you?' said Ivy. 'Well, no more do I. So – we get Ada down here. After all, it was her Jessie went to in the first place…' She looked at her husband and smiled wickedly. 'And we always said she ought to have a bit of a holiday – her and the kids…

75

didn't we?'

Sir Frederick sighed in mock exasperation. 'Yes, my dear.'

'And we have still got the house on Cliff Terrace?'

'Oh, Ivy!' protested Dorinda. 'Ada wouldn't know what to do with herself in that great house!'

Ivy grinned. 'Don't you worry about that, Miss! You just carry on giving the holidaymakers a good time. I'll let you know what's happening in a day or so. Come along, Freddie.'

And that, thought Dorinda with a smile, was that. She had simply intended to ask Ivy to ask Ada if she knew what went on in the disreputable halls in which Aramantha had been appearing – but Ivy, as usual, had other ideas. And, Dorinda had to admit, they were often good ones.

The following day there was no news from either Ivy or Inspector Colyer, and Jessie began to relax. Dorinda was impressed that her performances hadn't suffered throughout the recent problems, but she was aware that any small thing could tip the balance. The other girls were definitely happier without Aramantha, and Dorinda wondered what would happen if the girl turned up unharmed and wanting to come back. Would she take her?

'No,' said Maude, when this was put to her. 'She's let you down once too often, if you ask me. We shouldn't have taken her in the first place.'

'Last year?' Dorinda was shocked. 'I thought…'

'No, I mean this time.'

'But you were the one…'

Maude, rather pink in the face, lifted her chin. 'I know. I

was wrong.'

'Well, it's too late now. Perhaps we shouldn't have taken her back that first time – after Velda's death.'

'But that was the inspector's idea, wasn't it? And Ivy took her home with her for a few days. You didn't have much choice,' said Maude. 'Come on, now. Buck up – you've got the others to think of and a new week coming up. '

'I know. A new programme to sort out.' Dorinda shuffled the sheet music on her desk. 'I suppose I could use the same set as two weeks ago. The audiences will be different.'

'Except the ones here for the season,' said Maude.

'They don't come that often.' Dorinda smiled up at her friend. 'Usually!'

Every summer, the new middle classes liked to decamp to the seaside. The wealthiest would take suites at hotels, but most would hire a house and bring the entire household, servants and all. The menfolk and boys at school would come down for weekends, and the boys for the whole of the summer holidays. It was while Dorinda had been governess to Sir Frederick's granddaughter Julia that she had had become acquainted with Maude, Will, and Will's Wanderers, as they were then, when Sir Frederick had taken a house on Cliff Terrace, Nethergate, for the season.

The following day, Sunday, with the new programmes for the week ahead set and the sun shining overhead, Dorinda felt more optimistic. Just as she was about to change into her Silver Serenaders pierrot costume, the telephone rang. Eyeing it with some trepidation, Dorinda

77

approached it.

'Dolly, is that you?'

'Yes, Ivy. It's me.'

'You'll be pleased about this,' said Ivy, sounding triumphant. 'Ada and the kids are coming down to Cliff House! And we've got a suggestion.'

'Yes?'

'Well, see, what Freddie and I thought -' for that, read "I thought", Dorinda assumed, 'was that we could turn Cliff House into The Alexandrians' lodgings! What do you think of that?'

'I – I don't know!' Dorinda was taken aback.

'They could all be in one place, see, there's plenty of room – well, you remember that – and Ada used to be in the business so she understands. And they might talk to her.'

'Do you mean she would spy on them? Oh, I don't think I'd like that.'

'No, not *spy*, just be at their side. And it's closer than the lodgings they've got now, and cheaper.'

That, Dorinda knew, would be in the scheme's favour. Landladies were inclined to charge rather more for 'theatricals' than other people. Dorinda was sure Ivy was preparing to charge a merely nominal amount for Cliff House.

'It sounds like a good idea,' she said cautiously, 'but I don't see how it helps with our current problem.'

'People wouldn't be inclined to, well, run away. Feel safe, see.'

'You mean Jessie, don't you?' Dorinda thought for a moment. 'Do you think she might want to, then?'

'Wouldn't surprise me. What with Aramantha going. She might think – oh, I dunno. Someone's after her, too?'

'You think Aramantha thought someone was after her?'

'Well, o' course! So do you. And that Inspector Colyer.'

Dorinda had to admit that was true.

'When's Ada coming? And shall I suggest it to the company?'

'Yeah, you do that. I bet Jessie'll feel happier. They don't 'ave to, o' course. Ted and Algy might not want to. She's comin' tomorrer – Freddie's sendin' Billy to fetch 'er.' Ivy's accent was slipping, a sure sign that she was becoming excited. 'You ring me when you've 'ad a word.'

Dorinda changed into her costume and decided to wait until the interval to put Ivy's suggestion to the company. There weren't as many in the audience as it was a sunny Sunday afternoon, and, as it often happened, meant that the programme moved along at a slightly quicker pace, so Dorinda was able to deliver her news sooner than she had anticipated. It was greeted with surprised delight on all sides.

'All of us?' asked Ted. 'Even Algy and me?'

'All of you,' said Dorinda, 'but only if you want to. It will be cheaper, of course.'

There was unanimous approval of this.

'Ada?' said Jessie. 'I know Ada, don't I?'

'Yes, you do. Ivy's – I mean, Lady Ivy's sister.'

'Oh.' Jessie's face broke into a smile. 'I'd like that.'

'Well, you'll have to give notice to your current lodgings, so I expect it will be next week before you move – I doubt if Ada would be ready for you before then. But I'm glad you're pleased.' Dorinda went back to the office and just had time to put in a telephone call to Ivy to tell her the good news. She still wasn't sure that it was going to help with Jessie's situation, and even less with Aramantha's, but that, she decided, was now out of her hands and nothing to do with The Alexandrians.

CHAPTER ELEVEN

The landladies, it turned out, were more than happy to let their tenants leave as soon as they liked – with a full week's rent, of course – as it gave them time to have the rooms ready for the new influx of holidaymakers the following weekend. The week, therefore, was a flurry of activity. First, the arrival of Ada and the children, then Cliff House to be got ready which involved May, Ellen, and even Ivy arriving from Anderson Place to help. Finally, the gradual removal of The Alexandrians into their new home from home.

'Trouble is, Dolly,' said Maude, sitting down on an office chair and fanning herself with her apron, 'none of them will want to go home at the end of the season.'

'Nice house, isn't it?' said Dorinda, amused.

'Cut above any of the other lodgings,' said Maude. 'Even ours.' She looked pointedly at Dorinda, who laughed.

'There isn't room for us as well,' she said. 'Besides, they wouldn't want me there too. They'd feel I was spying on them.'

Since this was, in effect, what Ivy had suggested, she shifted uncomfortably in her seat.

'Oh, well,' sighed Maude, 'I'd better go and make sure the dressing rooms are ready – they'll never have time to do that themselves by the time they get down here.'

It was Thursday, and today the programme changed. Dorinda had written out the order of the items to be performed. She gave the lists to Maude and sat down to start on the seemingly inexhaustible pile of bills. She was so engrossed, she didn't see the approach down the slope of Inspector Jack Colyer, and answered his knock on the office door with a vague, 'yes?'

'Miss Alexander.'

Dorinda looked up and met the dark brown eyes. She swallowed convulsively.

'Inspector.' She stood up and smoothed down her skirt. 'Is – is there any news of Aramantha?'

He shook his head. 'She hasn't been seen, no. I take it you have no news either?'

'No.'

He placed his bowler carefully on the desk, leaning forward onto it . 'And where is Miss Jones? I have just come from her lodgings…'

'Ah.' Dorinda smiled in relief. 'Her *former* lodgings.'

He raised his eyebrows. 'Former?'

'Did the landlady not tell you?' Dorinda's smile was now tinged with mischief. 'How annoying for you.'

'Dorinda!' Colyer's tone held a warning note. She sat down again.

'We have moved the company into Cliff House.' She looked up at him.

'Lady Ivy's idea – partly to keep Jessie safe. She thought Jessie might still be in danger.'

Colyer frowned. 'How will moving lodgings keep her safer?'

'I'm not really sure either, but the whole company, including the men, have moved in there. Lady Ivy's sister Ada has come down to act as housekeeper.'

'So they have a dragon.' He perched on the edge of the desk and folded his arms. 'Is she supposed to keep Jessie Jones under lock and key?'

Dorinda was surprised. 'Of course not! Why would she do that?'

'To stop Jessie from leaving.' He narrowed his eyes at her. 'Don't tell me you haven't thought of that?'

Dorinda felt heat creeping into her cheeks.

'I see you have. You thought up this ingenious scheme to keep her under observation.'

'I did not!' Dorinda was indignant. 'It was all Lady Ivy's idea. Cliff House has been empty for a year because Sir Frederick didn't want to sell it -'

'I didn't realise he owned it.'

'Neither did I at first, but that's what's happened. The company are delighted. Why are you here?'

'I told you. I was looking for Jessie Jones.'

'Why?'

'We – the police - have some questions for her.'

Dorinda stood up and went to the window, then opened the door to the foyer.

'There are no other officers here.'

'I merely want to ask her a few questions.'

Dorinda eyed him doubtfully. 'In here?'

'If you don't mind.'

'Very well. I'll see if she's arrived yet. They no longer have to come down so early, you see.'

Now what? wondered Dorinda as she made her way backstage. Unsurprised to find no one there but Maude and Will, she returned to the office where the inspector stood staring out of the window.

'I'm sorry, no one's arrived yet. Would you like me to take you up to Cliff House?'

Colyer turned around. 'That might be – upsetting, don't you think?'

Surprised again at this delicacy, Dorinda nodded slowly. 'Well, do sit down. We can watch the slope from here and catch her when she comes in.'

After a moment, Colyer sat down and cleared his throat. 'I'm sorry if I seem to be pestering the young ladies...'

'Only one, at the moment,' said Dorinda.

'But we do need to find out where Ethel Small – sorry, Aramantha Giles – is.'

' Why should Jessie know?'

'That's what I need to find out,' said Colyer obscurely.

'Here come the girls,' said Dorinda, catching sight of the laughing group coming down Cliff Steps. 'They certainly like their new lodgings.'

Colyer stood up to watch them out of the window as they approached Victoria Place and the slope down to The Alexandria.

'Hmm,' he said, turning away to the door.

All signs of merriment died when the girls opened the main doors and caught sight of him.

'I'm sorry, Miss Jones,' he said formally. 'Could I have a few more words, please?'

Dorinda read panic in Jessie's face and stepped forward.

84

'Don't worry, Jessie. Would you like me to be with you?'
She ignored Colyer's frown.

'Yes, please,' Jessie whispered, and giving the other
girls an anxious look, followed Dorinda into the office.
Colyer came in and closed the door, pulling forward the
visitor's chair.

'Now, I just need to know if you ever came across
Aramantha Giles when you were in London.'

Jessie looked surprised. 'Aramantha? No – I'd never met
'er till I come down 'ere.'

'And could you tell me the names of the halls you
worked in?'

'But I told you last time!'

'Tell me again, please.' Colyer smiled. 'I didn't make a
note, and I've got a terrible memory.'

Dorinda gave an inward snort at this palpable untruth.

Jessie reeled off the names of the few small halls she had
been working in London. 'But why?'

'And that was all? You didn't work for any of the – shall
we say, the more private clubs?'

Jessie frowned. 'No – just the ones I said. I know there
was private clubs, but I – well, I 'eard they wasn't
very… nice.' Jessie's colour had risen. 'I wouldn't work in
them.'

'You don't know what they were called?'

Jessie looked bewildered. 'No.'

'Who told you about them?'

Now Jessie looked confused. 'What d'you mean, 'oo? I
dunno. Just girls…'

' No one ever approached you about them?'

'Approached?' By now Jessie's colour had risen even further.

'A gentleman, for instance.'

Jessie shook her head vigorously, but Dorinda was convinced she wasn't telling the truth. So, obviously, was the inspector.

'You said your step-father attacked you on your way home. He didn't mention these private clubs?'

'No!' Jessie stood up. 'I dunno nothin' about no clubs! I said.'

'Very well, Jessie.' He smiled at her again. 'That's all for the moment. Thank you.'

Jessie bolted from the room.

'She knows.' The inspector moved to the window once more. 'Let's hope she doesn't take it into her head to run as Ethel Small did.'

'Do you really think there's a connection between Aramantha and Jessie? I could swear they didn't know one another,' said Dorinda.

'I think the connection is Jessie's step-father. He attacked them both, after all.'

'I assumed he attacked Jessie because of her... profession.' Dorinda fidgeted uncomfortably. 'Because of his – what? Religious tendencies.'

'Do you really believe that's what it was? Oh, Dorinda!'

Colouring faintly, Dorinda met his eyes squarely. 'And just how would your questions help to find Aramantha?'

For a moment, Colyer looked confused.

'They wouldn't, would they? Or...' Dorinda thought. 'If she had known a name...'

'Exactly.'

'And her stepfather was connected to these private clubs?'

'I believe so. I think he wanted Jessie in there.'

'But… what about his Brother Anarawd activities? Were they all a lie?'

Colyer sat down on the visitor's chair. 'In a way, I don't think so. I think probably he truly was disgusted by the activities. Did either Aramantha or Jessie ever say anything to you they may not have said to me?'

'Well…' Dorinda reflected. 'Yes. Aramantha did. I didn't truly understand it. The man who attacked her whispered to her about sin and how he could save her. Then she said he couldn't do something.' She looked up at Colyer. 'Do *you* understand it?'

Oh, yes,' said Colyer after a moment. 'I understand.'

CHAPTER TWELVE

When Colyer left Dorinda stood up, collected her hat and jacket, and went to find Maude.

'I'm going up to Cliff House,' she said. 'I won't be long.'

'Why? What did that inspector say?' Maude looked worried.

'Not much. He wanted know if there was a link between Aramantha and Jessie.'

'Of course there isn't!' Maude was indignant. 'I can't imagine two girls more different.'

'I know.' Dorinda sighed. 'But I'm going up to find out if Ada knows anything – perhaps about - oh, I don't know. Something I don't. Is Jessie all right?'

'Not really. She isn't saying much, though.'

'Well, I trust you to keep an eye on her. Won't be long.'

Dorinda left the building and went quickly up the slope, crossed Victoria Place and climbed Cliff Steps. She could not prevent a shiver and a sensation of dread as she approached Cliff House, remembering her own time living there a few years ago, but resolutely suppressed it as she knocked sharply on the front door.

Ada opened it, revealing May behind her industriously sweeping the hallway.

'Hello, Ada!' said Dorinda brightly. 'And May – a bit

different to how it was, isn't it?'

'More cheerful-like, Miss!' May grinned. 'I'd be 'appy to stay 'ere now.'

'Oh, you wouldn't leave Lady Ivy and Sir Frederick, would you?' Dorinda laughed. 'And Mrs Nemone and Julia.'

' No, that I wouldn't!' May returned to her sweeping.

'Did you want to see me, Dolly?' Ada looked nervous.

'If you can spare me a minute.' Dorinda followed into the big drawing room on the left of the hall, which now looked as if it was Ada and the children's main living quarters.

'Nearer the kitchen down 'ere, see,' said Ada, 'and it leaves all the rooms upstairs for your girls and boys.'

'Very sensible, Ada.' Dorinda sat down on the edge of the sofa, a relic from its former days under the Shepherd and Anderson regime. Ada perched on an upright chair, looking anxious.

'Now, what I wanted to know was anything you could tell me about these places Jessie and Aramantha were working in before they came down here.'

Ada frowned. 'I don't know as I know much, Dolly. Oh, I know the small halls Jessie was playin', good ones, they was, but I dunno where Ethel – sorry, Aramantha - was. She musta told that inspector. Didn't she tell you?'

'No. I gather they were private clubs.' Dorinda looked down at her lap. 'Not very nice ones.'

'Oh.' Ada nodded, and relaxed. 'Well, I can't tell you much about *them*, but we all knew about 'em.'

'And the girls – were they actually performers?'

'Well, they danced a bit, far as I can tell, and maybe sang, but that wasn't what they were there for, if you know what I mean.'

'Yes, I thought so. Maude told me a bit about them. But I wondered if there was – anything else?'

'Anything else? 'Ow d'you mean?'

'I don't exactly know.' Dorinda leaned forward. 'But now Aramantha's run away – if she has – and Jessie seems to be so scared, well, I wondered. What they could be so scared of.'

'I think it's *'oo* they're scared of,' said Ada, after a moment's thought. 'See, these places ain't legal, like, and the people runnin' 'em – well, you wouldn't want to get on their wrong side, if you know what I mean.'

'So these clubs – or whatever they are – the men running them are criminals. Yes, I think I'd realised that.' Dorinda tapped her lips with a forefinger. 'And girls who run away are punished?'

'Oh, yes. Far as I can say.'

'But Jessie hasn't worked for them…'

'No – but maybe they was trying to get her to work for them,' suggested Ada.

'And she ran away to avoid it?'

'I dunno.' Ada shrugged. 'When she first come to me, she'd bin given the push 'cos of her pa and all them women carryin' banners.'

'And he'd attacked her.' Dorinda frowned. 'And now he's dead.' She looked up at Ada. 'I don't see the link at all, do you?'

'But Ethel – Aramantha – said 'e was one o' the men in

the club, didn't she? Ivy said -'

'At first she said she didn't know who attacked her,' said Dorinda. She sighed. 'Do you think there was more going on in those places than just the – well, the girls? That if they knew about it...'

'But Jessie didn't work in them places,' insisted Ada. 'I'm sure she didn't.'

'So was I, but now I'm wondering.'

'Oh, don't, Dolly! She wouldn't! They might've been tryin' to make 'er, but I swear she didn't.'

'No, I didn't think so, either. But it's so puzzling.' Dorinda stood up. 'And worrying. Well, Ada, if Jessie – or even one of the others – says anything you think might help, will you let me know?'

Ada looked doubtful. 'I don't like spyin', Dolly...'

'No, I don't want you to do that. We just need to find out what happened to those girls, don't we?'

Ada stood up. 'Oh, yes. It's shockin' what some men do. I'll listen out.'

When Dorinda got back to The Alexandria she was just in time to change for the afternoon performance. The weather had clouded over and the house was packed with people taking shelter from the promise of rain. Despite what might be going on under the surface the company, including Jessie, performed well up to standard. At the end, after the final chorus, Dorinda went to congratulate them.

She had barely had time to say, 'well done', when Maude came bursting in.

'Dolly – there's someone to see you.'

'Who? Not the inspector again?'

'No.' Maude looked puzzled. 'It's a man. Well, a gentleman, I suppose. He said he wanted to see the manager.'

'Oh?' Dorinda raised her eyebrows. 'Did you tell him who the manager was?'

'No.' Maude grinned. 'Be a bit of a surprise, won't it?'

'Shall I come with you, Dolly?' Will came forward.

'Maybe just to the foyer, Will? Thank you.'

The auditorium doors were still closed, and Dorinda motioned Will through while she and Maude remained where they were.

As Will entered the foyer, a well-dressed man rose from the seats ranged against the wall.

'Good afternoon,' he said, in a soft cultured voice. 'I would like to speak to the proprietor of this concert party. As I am in a similar way of business in London, I am sure we would have much to say to each other.'

'Yes, sir.' Will kept a straight face and opened the auditorium doors. 'Allow me to present Miss Alexander.'

Dorinda stepped forward and the man's jaw dropped.

'Miss…?' he repeated, in a strangled gasp.

'I am the proprietor,' said Dorinda. 'How may I assist you?'

The man closed his mouth with a snap. 'But -' he began, and stopped.

'If you have some business with me, perhaps we should step into the office.' Dorinda opened the door. 'Maude, perhaps you would accompany us?'

The man cleared his throat. 'Er – I think I may have been misinformed,' he said quickly. 'I am sorry to have bothered you.' And without another word, he whipped round and through the main doors.

'Well!' said Dorinda. 'What do you make of that?'

Will was scowling. 'Whatever it was, it wasn't fit for a woman's ears.'

'No.' Dorinda nodded. 'But what?'

Maude shook her head. 'He wanted a woman, of course. One of ours.'

'How do you know?' Dorinda was shocked.

'Obvious, isn't it? He comes to see the manager and when he finds it's a woman he scarpers.'

'But surely,' said Dorinda, thinking hard, 'a female proprietor of a concert party could be just as dishonourable as a male one? Think of all the women...'

'Yes, dear, I know.' Maude patted her arm. 'But ladies aren't suppose to know about things like that, are they?'

'Women who run concert parties do,' said Dorinda grimly.

'You know what I think?' said Will. 'I think Aramantha was working in one of those Night Houses.'

'They was done away with over twenty years ago, Will,' said Maude repressively.

'What are Night Houses?' asked Dorinda.

Maude frowned a 'now see what you've done' frown at her husband and ushered Dorinda into the office.

'Night houses, duck,' she said, sitting opposite Dorinda at the desk, 'were like regular clubs. All posh, like, chandeliers, everything. But they were for one reason and one reason only.'

'And they've been stopped?' Now it was Dorinda's turn

to frown. 'But...'

'They weren't regular brothels, Dolly, and yes, I know there are still brothels, but they're illegal, aren't they? Well so are Night Houses. You know the Act twenty-odd years ago? Made all that sort of thing illegal, but it's reckoned they just went underground. A lot of them – well, they weren't...' Maude was obviously searching for the right word.

'So you knew about them when Aramantha first turned up?'

'I told you. Will and I were taken to a couple that were supposed to be regular old-fashioned halls. We reckoned we knew what they were.'

'And this was where Aramantha was.' Dorinda frowned. She looked up at Maude. 'But you think it was worse than just... that. Men wanting women.'

Maude nodded slowly.

'Are you going to tell me?' asked Dorinda.

'I can't, Dolly.' Maude had turned a flustered pink.

Dorinda watched her thoughtfully for a minute. 'I see,' she said finally. 'And do you think that gentleman has something to do with one of those places?'

Maude shrugged. 'Could be. Scared of something, wasn't he? He said he was in a similar way of business.'

'But he meant a concert party,' said Dorinda.

'Did he?' said Will. 'I'm not so sure of that.'

Dorinda nodded slowly. 'Do you think I should tell Inspector Colyer?'

'I don't know, Dolly. Maybe.'

After Maude had left the office, Dorinda sat for a long

time staring at the telephone. Thoughts were tumbling around her head in complete confusion, and the only way she could think of sorting them into some kind of order, was to tell Jack Colyer.

CHAPTER THIRTEEN

Will went with Maude to buy the pies that afternoon. Were they all getting worried, wondered Dorinda? She had tried to minimise speculation about Aramantha, the murder and the frequent visits from the police, but it was inevitable that the unease would spread.

She watched as Will and Maude reappeared at the top of the slope and started in surprise as she realised that following behind was Constable Fred Fowler. He wheeled his bicycle down the slope instead of chaining it to the railings as usual. Was he becoming nervous, too?

She was seated once more behind the desk when Maude brought her pie in.

'Will told Fred,' she announced, with a slightly defiant air. 'He's come down to have a word.'

'All right, Maudie.' Dorinda smiled at her lieutenant. 'Send him in.'

Constable Fred sidled into the office, clapping his helmet in front in him.

'Will and Maude told you about the gentleman who came to see us earlier, did they, Constable?' Dorinda knew better than to ask him to sit. He never did.

'Yes, Miss.' He frowned. 'They wasn't sure what he wanted.'

'No. He wouldn't say.' Dorinda gazed wistfully at her

rapidly cooling pie. 'He was disconcerted when he realised that I was the owner of the company.'

'He – what?'

'He was surprised. We thought he'd come to ask for something, but when he realised I was a woman, he turned tail and left.'

'What would he want?' asked Fred. Then he stopped and frowned again. 'Oh, I see.' He nodded wisely. 'People still think it's not quite right, don't they?'

'Do they? Oh – I see what you mean! Some people still think all actresses and dancers are no better than they should be. Yes, that's true, but I think he wanted something specific – I mean,' she corrected herself hastily, 'something *special*.'

'But…' began Constable Fred. He stopped and shook his head. 'I dunno, Miss. Some o' the things I've heard about – they don't seem natural, to me. Is that what you're thinking?'

'Probably,' said Dorinda, not at all sure what exactly she was thinking.

'I think I'd better tell the inspector.' Fred put back his shoulders decisively. 'Before he goes back to London.'

'Has he been staying down here?' asked Dorinda, feeling a definite sense of relief.

'At The Albion, Miss. Very respectable house. If you'll pardon me, I'll just go and see if I can catch him.'

'I hope you do, Constable,' said Dorinda. She watched him out of the door, and as he laboriously pushed his bicycle up the slope, before falling hungrily on her pie.

It was unsurprising, then, that shortly before the evening

performance was due to start, Colyer himself appeared in the foyer.

'I'm just about to go on,' Dorinda told him, with her hand on the auditorium door.

'Your mysterious guest of this afternoon isn't in the audience, is he?' Colyer asked.

'No, Maude would have told me straight away – she sees everyone in. Can I go now?'

'Don't let any of the young ladies go home on their own tonight,' he said abruptly, and left.

Dorinda worried about this admonition with half her brain, while concentrating on the slightly below-par performance of the company with the other. Hardly surprising, she thought, that they were unnerved, although the three men were as cheerfully brash as ever. At the end of the evening she made sure that they all left together, and she, Maude and Will watched them go up the slope, cross to Cliff Steps and eventually up the steps to the door of Cliff House.

'Much easier to keep an eye on them,' said Will with a nod of satisfaction, turning to check the inside of The Alexandria and the back door to the outside gallery.

'I just wish we didn't have to keep an eye on them,' said Dorinda, skewering her hat onto her head.

'Mmm.' Maude was still staring up at Victoria Place.

'What's the matter?' Dorinda turned to look at her friend. 'What have you seen?'

'Oh – nothing.' Maude pulled herself together with a slight shake of her head. 'I was just wondering if we could have kept Aramantha any safer if they'd already moved to

Cliff House.'

'I don't see how,' said Dorinda. 'After all, she seems to have left of her own accord, hasn'tshe?'

'But someone might have seen her. *We* might have done.'

'Yes,' said Dorinda doubtfully, 'but we wouldn't have been watching, would we?'

'No.' Maude heaved a sigh as Will rejoined them.

'Come on, then. Let's go home.'

By Friday morning the weather had changed from the typical June sunshine of the previous few days to cloudy grey skies, and sea whipped to ice cream peaks along the shoreline. Dorinda left the lodgings early, intending to call in at Cliff House to see if Ada had anything to report. However, on her way towards Cliff Terrace she was surprised to see Constable Robert pedalling furiously towards her along the high street.

'Constable?' she said, as he came to a breathless halt in front of her. 'Have you any news?'

'Not exactly, Miss,' he panted. 'But Inspector Colyer wanted to tell you, Miss, that we've got a boy reported missing.'

'Oh?' Dorinda was bewildered. 'I'm sorry, of course…'

'No – see, it's not that!' Constable Robert was struggling. 'He said – the inspector, that is – it was important. He said you needed to know.'

'And he didn't say why?'

'No, Miss!' Now Constable Robert looked as bewildered as Dorinda. Clearly, he had expected her to know the relevance of the missing boy.

'All right, Constable, you can tell him you've told me.' Dorinda smiled at the perspiring constable, who thankfully remounted his bicycle and pedalled more slowly off in the direction of the police station.

Dorinda continued in the direction of Cliff Terrace, thinking hard. Why was a missing boy relevant to either the murder of Brother Anarawd or the disappearance of Aramantha?

When Ada opened the door to Dorinda's knock, it was clear that she had news to import.

'That policeman's been 'ere,' she announced, before Dorinda had even spoken.

'About a missing boy?' Dorinda was sorry to take the wind out of Ada's sails, as she saw the latter's face fall.

'Yeah – how did you know?'

'I met Constable Fowler Junior on the high street. He was coming to tell me.'

'But why?' Ada pulled Dorinda inside. 'Come in the kitchen – do you mind?'

'No, of course not.'

Dorinda followed down the long dark hall and down the steps into the kitchen, where it was even darker.

'Why did the inspector come here?' Dorinda asked, as she settled herself at the huge scrubbed table.

'To warn us. But as I told 'im, we ain't got no boys, 'ave we?' Dorinda had to hide a smile at the 'we'. In all of four days, Ada had identified herself completely with The Alexandrians.

'No, Ada, we haven't. But what is it about boys? We don't get boys in music hall at all, do we?'

Ada looked away. 'N-no...'

'What is it? Come on, Ada, you know something.'

'It's just... well,' Ada turned back to Dorinda and continued in a rush, 'you remember we all told you about the sort of places Ethel – Aramantha – was workin'?'

Dorinda nodded.

'Well, see, it wasn't only women...' Ada was now regarding Dorinda with fearful eyes.

Dorinda felt the colour recede from her face as the blood drained from her head. She felt almost faint for a moment and had to look down at her hands gripping the edge of the table, until everything swam back into focus.

'You all right, Dolly?' Ada's anxious voice reached through the fog.

'Yes.' Dorinda managed to look up. She took a deep breath and nodded. 'You mean it wasn't just women men went there for?'

Ada shook her head.

'Other men?'

'Not just men.' Ada's voice was now just a whisper.

'Oh, God.' Dorinda put her head in her hands.

'I'm sorry, Dolly.' Dorinda felt Ada's warm hand on her shoulder. ''Ere, I'll get us a cup o' tea.'

By the time there was a cup of strong, dark brown tea in front of her, Dorinda had recovered. 'Tell me, Ada, does everybody know about this sort of thing?'

Ada looked uncomfortable. 'Well, everyone 'oo's in the business. Everyone knows all the villains in London 'ang around the 'Alls. It don't get talked about, like, but people knows.'

'So all my girls know?'

Ada nodded again. 'I don't say as they know the ins and outs like, but they know it 'appens.'

'And Aramantha definitely knew,' said Dorinda.

'Oh, yes. You've only got to remember what she and Martha used to do.'

Dorinda had every reason to remember this episode from last year's season.

'She ran away then, too, didn't she?'

'It wasn't exactly runnin' away, was it?' said Ada. 'An' we dunno if she's run away this time, either.'

'Oh, don't say that!' moaned Dorinda.

'Anyways, I still dunno why that inspector wanted to warn us. I mean, it ain't like it is at 'ome, is it?' Ada gazed out of the barred window at the feet of people walking along Cliff Terrace.

'No.' Dorinda stood up. 'Will you tell the girls – and Ted and Algy – what the inspector said?'

'O 'course,' said Ada. 'You sure you're all right, Dolly?'

'Yes, thank you, Ada.' In truth, Dorinda admitted to herself that she still felt somewhat shaky, and as she climbed the steps from the basement door to Cliff Terrace she had to take several deep breaths. Her imagination was still refusing to come to terms with what Ada had told her, but she knew it would come back to haunt her.

She was surprised, as she descended Cliff Steps, to see a small band of Brother Anarawd's former followers, including the women she thought of as Short and Tall, gathered together near the top of the slope to The Alexandria.

'Not again,' she muttered under her breath.

'Miss Alexander.'

Dorinda stopped in surprise.

'I hear one of your employees has gone missing.' Short regarded her with malevolently bright eyes. 'Just after Brother Anarawd was murdered.'

Rightly guessing the inference she was supposed to draw, Dorinda refused to do so.

'Yes,' she said brightly. 'One hopes that the murderer hasn't killed our Miss Giles, too.'

Short opened her mouth but no sound came out, only a look of surprised hatred in her eyes. Predictably, Tall uttered a low moan.

'And perhaps this boy, too?' said Short, recovering her tongue.

Dorinda inclined her head. 'Do excuse me,' she said politely, and set off down the slope.

Slightly unnerved by this encounter, Dorinda spent the next couple hours trawling through bills and accounts and wishing she could afford to pay someone else to do it. The rest of the company filtered in, but Dorinda could not bring herself to discuss what Ada had said with any of them, even Maude. Eventually, the afternoon's audience began to arrive, and Dorinda donned her pierrot costume then made her way through the auditorium, acknowledged the smattering of applause with a small bow and took her seat at the piano. Throughout the first half of the programme she endeavoured to put all her worries about small boys, Jessie, and Aramantha out of her mind, although she only partly succeeded. It was when Jessie came on in her guise as the urchin that she suddenly sat up with a start, almost losing her place in the song. Jessie cast her a nervous look from the stage, but carried on valiantly until she left the stage to resume her pierrot costume for the last chorus before the interval.

Dorinda played the final chord, once again acknowledged the applause, and hurried round to the dressing room area.

'Jessie,' she said, stopping the girl as she was about to start her change into evening dress. 'I'm sorry about that – just now. I had a thought.'

'Oh?' Jessie looked nervous. 'It doesn't matter…'

'No – listen.' Dorinda sat down on one of the huge costume trugs and pulled Jessie down beside her. 'Did you perform that urchin song in London?'

'Yes,' said Jessie. 'Why?'

'Did you perform any others as a child? Say, as a schoolboy? Or a cabin boy?'

'Yes – I did the schoolboy and a climber.'

'Climber?' echoed Dorinda.

'Chimney sweep's boy,' said Betty, making Dorinda aware that the whole company was listening.

'Did you want me to do some different songs, then?' asked Jessie. 'Only I ain't got the music for 'em – we'd 'ave to work it out like we did for the others.'

'No.' Dorinda patted her hand. 'I'd like to hear them, though. Carry on and get changed.'

Jessie dived behind the screen as if she couldn't get away fast enough, and Maude took her place. 'What's up?' she murmured. 'What's upset you?'

'I was just thinking,' said Dorinda, 'about what you said about people wanting something different.' She glanced quickly sideways. 'And I thought about…' She took a deep breath. 'Well, Jessie singing songs as a small boy.'

Maude stared. 'What do you know about that?' she whispered eventually. 'About – boys?'

'Not very much. But I know there were men who…' She stopped.

'And men who found them.' Maude sounded vicious.

'But it all stopped, didn't it?' Dorinda knew what the answer would be, but she couldn't help asking.

'The same as everything else, I expect. Went underground.' Maude was looking at the floor now. 'I always thought we'd be away from it all down here. You know, clean air, nice people…'

'Instead you found it was just like everywhere else,' said Dorinda with a sigh.

'More or less.' Maude looked up and gave her a crooked grin. 'It's not so bad, really – although we do seem to have got into trouble a few times, don't we?'

'Oh, we have, Maudie, we have.' Dorinda sighed again. 'And all since you met me.'

CHAPTER FOURTEEN

'What do you know about it?' Maude repeated. 'Who told you?'

'I asked Ada. The inspector had been to warn her – and the company – that the boy was missing.'

'Why? What's it got to do with us?" said Maude in surprise.

'That's what Ada said – because we haven't got any boys, and I said, well, you didn't have boys in music hall or concert parties. So, then she told me. Reluctantly, but she told me. That's what I suddenly thought of while Jessie was doing her Urchin number.'

Maude frowned. 'What do you mean? Men might want her because she dresses up?'

'Well, yes.' Dorinda felt the heat creeping into her cheeks again. 'I don't know what they like, or want, and I don't even want to think about it, but it makes a sort of sense.'

'What about her step-pa? He was against her, wasn't he?' Maude looked puzzled. 'Oh – wait! But he attacked her…'

'Exactly. He wasn't what he pretended to be at all, was he? Remember, Aramantha identified him as the man who frightened her, too.' Dorinda looked thoughtful. 'And that's odd, too, because if she was in those – what did you call them? – Night Houses, she must have known…' she looked quickly at Maude and then away again, 'well, she must have. Mustn't she?'

'Oh, she knew all right. As I said, remember what she and that Velda used to get up to.'

'So she must have been scared of something else,' said Dorinda. ' Is that why she's run away now?'

'Well,' said Maude, standing up, 'let's hope she 'as run away, or else she's been taken.'

Dorinda went slowly back to the piano ready to start the second half, waiting while the audience filtered in to resume their seats. She found herself scrutinising them far more closely than usual, especially the men, and at the end of the show she made sure she was in the foyer ready to see them all out. Maude raised her eyebrows but made no comment until she had shut the doors on the last customer.

'What was that about?' she asked.

'I just wanted to see what they were like.' Dorinda went into the office. 'And now I'm going to go to Fat Aggie's to get the pies.'

'You? Why?'

'I need a breath of air.'

'Not you! Come on, what is it?' Maude planted herself in front of the office door.

Dorinda turned to face her. 'I want to see if those women are still there, and to see if Aggie's heard any more about that missing boy.'

'I could do that.'

'I know you could.' Dorinda took off her tall hat and shook out her hair. 'But I want to go.'

'All right, but don't go getting into mischief,' said Maude reluctantly.

Dorinda burst out laughing. 'I'll try not to, mother!'

Fat Aggie's shop was a faithful recreation of her family's London pie and mash shop; it served nearly the same food without the heavy emphasis on eels, as surprisingly, down here on the coast, they were not as plentiful as they were in London. Dorinda loved it, not least because it was the very last place a lady would be expected to be seen.

Fat Aggie greeted her cheerfully. 'Don't often see you 'ere, love. 'Ow are yer?'

Dorinda smiled. 'I'm well, Aggie. How are you?'

'Apart from me feet, I'm grand. The usual is it?'

'Yes, please. And I wanted to ask you a couple of questions, if you don't mind.'

Aggie looked at her shrewdly. 'About them Bible thumpers, is it? Cor, they don't 'arf put off trade.'

'Well, partly. They were around again this morning – and I thought the police had sent them packing after the murder.'

Aggie shrugged. 'Not seen 'em this afternoon. Course, some o' them were local – coulda gone 'ome.'

'Local?' Dorinda was surprised. 'Weren't they all from London?'

'Nah. Only them ringleaders, like. The bloke wot got done and 'is two women. Women! Ha!' Aggie snorted. 'Two dried-up ol' prunes, they was.'

'Oh, I see. So where did all the others come from?'

'Round and about. Always be folk 'appy to join in,

won't there?'

'Yes,' said Dorinda, 'but a couple of my customers said they'd seen them in London outside the Music Halls.'

'Same people?'

'Well, I thought that's what they meant, but I suppose they might have meant just people protesting.'

'Like them at 'Yde Park.' Aggie burst into fat chuckles. 'Cor – should 'ear some o' them! Or p'raps you 'ave?'

'No, but I wish I had.' Dorinda started counting out money on to Aggie's high marble counter. 'I used to live in London.'

'I know yer did, luvvie. With Ivy and Sir Freddie, an' that poor Mrs Shepherd.'

'I realise now there was a lot I didn't understand about the world then.' Dorinda looked up at Aggie's smiling face. 'But I bet you do! Have you heard any more about that missing child?'

Aggie's face immediately became solemn. ''E ain't bin found.'

'I don't know much about it,' said Dorinda. 'It was a boy, wasn't it? Was he a holidaymaker?'

'Nah. Joe Briggs's boy.'

'Joe Briggs?'

'Fishin'. Boy goes with 'im.' Aggie shook her head. 'Sleeps in the nettin' shed when 'is dad's 'ad a few.'

'Oh, poor child! How old is he?'

'I dunno – could be ten, twelve.'

'When was he found to be missing?'

'Joe went to wake 'im up this morning to go out on the tide an''e weren't there. No sign of 'im.' Aggie shook her head again. 'I reckon 'e's run orf.'

'You don't think someone would have taken him, then?'

'Taken 'im?' scoffed Aggie. 'Wot for? Joe ain't got no money.'

'No, I suppose not.' Dorinda felt vaguely ashamed of what she had been thinking. Why would one boy be taken down here in Nethergate, where there were no Night Houses... or were there? She realised that what she had said earlier about not understanding the world was right. She knew nothing about whatever underworld Nethergate had.

She paid Aggie, picked up her warm, savoury-smelling parcel and left the shop, pausing to stand by the railings to look down on the beach. All she knew about her adopted town was what she had been allowed to see by her protectors. First Maude, Will, and the Wanderers, then Sir Frederick, Ivy and Mrs Shepherd, and then Maude and Will again. She saw nothing that didn't pertain to the running of The Alexandria, saw no one who wasn't connected to it in some way – the concert party itself, the Anderson household and those on the periphery of her life: the landladies, the tradesmen and women, and the policemen. During the winter, she gave piano lessons at her lodgings and performed at the occasional party, such as the one at Anderson Place. She never went to parties herself, or socialised in any way, and for the first time for some years she suddenly wondered what she might have been missing. Perhaps she might be more in touch with the town and its people – Maude, Will, and Aggie obviously were. She also realised with a slight shock that she didn't even know what was going on in her own business, as had been amply demonstrated over the last two seasons. She had now been made aware of some of the less palatable fringes, and the revelations had made her aware of how unfitted her former life had made her for this one. No wonder everyone was so shocked on meeting her for the first time.

The smell of the pies brought her back to the present and she turned and walked slowly back to The Alexandria. Perhaps she really ought to think about leaving the business? But what would she do? Piano lessons and the odd party would not make enough money to keep her, and what about The Alexandrians? The company, and the building itself. She had talked grandly to Maude about installing proper seating and perhaps even a gallery. Was she ready to give that up?

As she paused at the top of the slope and looked down at The Alexandria, its cupola gleaming in the late afternoon sun, she knew she wasn't. She would just have to find a way to keep more up to date with all aspects of her chosen business, including the less savoury elements, and possibly be more wary about whom she allowed in – both to the company and her life. She must try and take part more in the life of her town. Perhaps even go to London for the winter, as all the others did.

As if the thought had conjured him up, she wasn't surprised to see Jack Colyer come out of the big front doors. He stood waiting as she slowly descended the slope.

'Collecting the supper?' he asked as she drew level with him. 'I thought Maude did that.'

'I wanted to speak to Fat Aggie.'

'Fat Aggie?'

'It's her pie shop. It's lovely,' said Dorinda wistfully.

'You want to own a pie shop, now?' said Colyer, sounding amused.

'No, of course not.' Dorinda lifted her chin. 'I must take these in. I gather you wanted to talk to me Or perhaps Jessie and the girls?'

'You, mainly.' Colyer opened the door for her. 'Shall I wait here?'

'You can wait for me in the office. The door isn't locked.'

Dorinda took the pies to the dressing room area, then took one out for herself and wrapped it in a piece of the greaseproof paper. When she returned to the office, it was to find Colyer standing by the window and Ivy seated before the desk, Maude standing beside her.

'They were already here,' said Colyer.

'Ivy?' Dorinda went to her seat behind the desk. 'Is something the matter?'

'Amy and me wanted to know what's going on,' said Ivy. 'You ''eard – heard – any more from Aramantha?'

'You think she's run away, too?' said Dorinda, glancing over at Colyer.

'Well, she ain't bin took – hasn't been taken,' said Ivy, her accent betraying her agitation.

'What do you think has happened to her, Lady Ivy?' asked Colyer, coming forward to the edge of the desk.

'I dunno. She would'na gone back, would she?'

'To where she was working in London? I thought she ran away from there, though?'

'She did,' said Dorinda. 'But it wasn't the place itself, it was one of the men – I told you.'

'But she identified the murder victim here as that person,' said Colyer. 'Might she have decided it was safe to go back?'

The four of them looked at each other in puzzlement.

'But she was so scared,' said Dorinda eventually. 'Really panic-stricken. Would just one man have done that? Besides, she said…' She stopped. She couldn't repeat what Aramantha had said. She didn't even really understand it herself.

Maude nodded. 'Makes it even more strange really, doesn't it Dolly?'

'What?' Ivy turned and looked up at Maude, who indicated the inspector with a jerk of her head.

'I've heard it all before, ladies,' he said with a slight smile, 'but if you want to explain, Maude - Mrs Beddowes – I'll step outside.'

'So what did she say to you, Dolly?' asked Maude, as soon as the door closed behind him.

'She said…' She paused. 'She said he couldn't. Just that – he couldn't.'

Ivy nodded wisely. 'Get it up. That's what she meant, didn't she, Maudie?'

'That's it, dear. And it's exactly what young Jessie told me, too.'

'She didn't say anything to me!' protested Dorinda.

'Look, luvvie.' Ivy leant forward and took one of Dorinda's hands across the desk. 'Course she wouldn't. You're different. Class, see? There are some things they can't tell you.'

Once again, it flashed across Dorinda's mind how deeply out of her depth she was in this business.

'Can you tell the inspector that? I think he ought to know,' she said eventually. 'I gather it means he couldn't – er – he couldn't...'

'Rape her,' Ivy finished for her succinctly.

'Yes,' said Dorinda, feeling her face flaming.

'Tell you what,' said Maude decisively, 'I'll get Will to tell him. I'll just go and fetch him.'

Ivy and Dorinda looked at each other helplessly after she'd gone.

'What difference do you think it makes?' asked Dorinda. ' What was the inspector here for, anyway?'

'Don't you know?'

'He just said he wanted to speak to me. I asked if he wanted the girls – Jessie in particular – but he said mainly me.'

'And what,' asked Ivy shrewdly, 'have you been doing to make him mad this time?'

'Nothing. I've been asking if people know anything about this boy that's disappeared – did you know about that?'

'No – what boy?'

'I asked Fat Aggie. She said it's a local fisherman's boy, maybe ten years old. I couldn't help thinking about those boys -' She stopped, unable to go on.

'And 'ow did you find out about 'em?' asked Ivy.

'I asked Ada. The inspector had been to see her and warned her. I wanted to know why.'

'And she told yer!' Ivy was angry, her accent slipping.

'I'll kill 'er!'

'She couldn't refuse to tell me, could she? '

'But you're not – what I mean ter say, is, well…'

'I don't belong here,' said Dorinda bluntly. 'That's the point, isn't it?'

Ivy's jaw dropped.

'I've been thinking about it since this morning,' continued Dorinda. 'I realised how I've been protected from real life ever since that business…'

'When you ran away,' said Ivy, back in control of herself.

'Yes. And how I've had protection ever since. You and Sir Freddie, Will and Maude – you've all protected me, and it wasn't until last year, first with Velda and Aramantha and then with Amy, that I began to see the -' she searched for a word.

'Real world,' Ivy finished for her. 'You're right. You're a different class, see. Oh, we all get used to it in the men – they can slum it with the best of us – but the women don't. Unless you're born into that class – like me, f'r instance – you won't understand it.'

Dorinda nodded sadly. 'That's what I was thinking. Perhaps I should give it all up.'

'What?' Ivy looked horrified. 'Don't you bloody dare!'

'But if I don't understand it -'

'Look - there's no need for you to understand what goes on with all the pimps and villains, is there? As long as me and Maudie and Will's around. *We* know – proved it, haven't we – and we can make sure it don't touch you or The Alexandria. Can't say we done much good this time, but at least we got young Jessie outta the way.'

'Did we, though?' said Dorinda. 'It looks as though her stepfather, or whoever he was, followed her down here anyway and then got murdered here.'

'Yeah – but why?' said Ivy. 'If he couldn't get it up – beggin' yer pardon, Dolly – why did 'e bother?' Ivy's accent had slipped right back into the East End now. She was on familiar ground.

'Come to that,' said Dorinda, 'why did he even bother to try again? If he – he couldn't.'

'Always thought it'd be better next time?' suggested Ivy. 'Yer never know, do yer?'

Maude came back into the office, her colour slightly heightened, followed by Will and Inspector Colyer.

'Turns out we needn't have bothered, Dolly,' said Maude. 'Seems he already knew.'

CHAPTER FIFTEEN

'I spoke with them both, Miss Alexander, if you remember. They were less inhibited with me than they were with you.' Colyer resumed his place at the window.

Dorinda put her head in her hands. 'Oh, God,' she said. 'See, Ivy? I told you.'

'See what?' asked Maude.

'Don't matter, Maudie,' said Ivy sharply. 'Bein' silly, that's all.'

Silence fell, until Ivy said briskly, 'that pie'll be stone cold, Dolly. You better eat up and get changed.'

Everyone moved, except the inspector.

'I need a word with Miss Alexander if you don't mind,' he said, ushering the other three out of the office. 'I won't keep her long.'

Dorinda eyed him nervously.

'What do you want?' she asked when he had closed the door behind an obviously reluctant Maude.

'To explain something to you.' He took up his familiar perch on the edge of the desk.

'What?'

He looked down at his clasped hands. 'Sometimes it's difficult to put it into plain words.'

Dorinda sighed. 'Because I don't fit into this world?'

He looked startled. 'Why do you say that?'

'Because it has been borne in upon me very forcibly today.' Dorinda stared past him and out of the window. 'In fact, I was discussing with Lady Ivy just now the possibility of leaving The Alexandria.'

He was silent for a moment. 'But what would you do?' he asked eventually.

'I don't know.'

'Tell me why. What happened today that made you feel this way?'

'I went to see Ada this morning.' Dorinda brought her eyes back to him. 'After you had been to see her.'

'Yes?' His face tightened.

'You told both of us about the missing child. Well, Constable Robert actually told me – and he didn't know why, either. So, I asked Ada and she explained about what happens in London.' She dropped her eyes.

'Did she now.'

'And I thought… I wondered… well, Jessie performs as a boy…'

He was quiet for so long, Dorinda thought she might have offended him. At last, he spoke.

'There are, unfortunately, some people who have a taste for that sort of thing.' He paused. 'Both men and women.'

'What?' Dorinda felt as if she couldn't take any more shocks.

'As far as our enquiries in London can ascertain, Jessie was not involved in anything other than straightforward performances at some smaller halls.'

'Good,' Dorinda forced the word from a dry throat. 'But she's still here. Aramantha isn't.'

118

'Quite.' Colyer cleared his throat and stood up.

'And why was she so frightened of that man? When she first arrived. She must have been used to – to -'

'I'm sure she was. It was the threat of death she was so scared of.'

'Death?' Dorinda's eyes became wide. 'Not…?'

'I wish I didn't have to tell you, Dorinda.' Colyer reached out and took her hands. 'I'm fairly sure you knew – or were told – that there were rumours about Aramantha Giles and Velda being too close?' He put his head on one side. 'And even Mrs Coutts and Mariah Belting?'

Dorinda's face was flaming as she stood up. 'Vicious rumours.'

'Certainly those regarding Mrs Coutts were, but I doubt that those about Aramantha and Velda were.' He shook her hands very slightly. 'Even if you don't know exactly…'

'What happens,' croaked Dorinda, freeing her hands.

'You can guess. And in some of those places where Aramantha was working, people – men – paid to see just that.'

Dorinda sat down again abruptly. 'I can't take any more.'

'I'm sorry, Dorinda, but you must be aware that if anyone involved in that world tries to break out of it, they will be in danger.'

'And you think that's what's happened to Aramantha?'

'I think that's what she feared, certainly.'

'But I still don't see what the disappearance of the child has to with us – or her?'

'The police know a lot about the people and places

Brother Anarawd, or Michael Evans, knew and frequented, and it is quite probable that those people now know about The Alexandria.'

Something was happening to Dorinda's stomach. The sensation of panic was almost overwhelming.

'And the trade in boys – sorry – will always overlap in their business. We just need to make sure these people aren't transferring their operation down here.'

Dorinda was transfixed.

'So I needed to warn you, and the rest of the cast, to be on their guard,' Colyer continued. 'It could simply be that the child has run off, but there are multiple examples of child kidnap in London -'

'Oh, please don't say Nethergate is becoming as bad as London!'

'I don't think so – not yet, anyway. No doubt as it grows, it might.'

'Grows?'

'Well, of course. It's already growing. There are far more people here now than there were in the nineties.'

'What shall I do, then?' Dorinda asked after a pause.

'Try and keep alert, don't go out on your own – any of you.'

'And about The Alexandria? You must see that I'm a bad fit for this sort of life.'

Colyer smiled. 'But you know what you're doing, even if you're not always aware of what's going on under the surface. And would you be happy?'

Dorinda looked down. 'Ivy thinks I should stay.'

'So do I.' Colyer leant across the desk and planted a soft

kiss on her lips. 'We'll all look after you.'

Dorinda was too surprised to protest and let him walk out of the office without saying another word.

'How?' she muttered to herself when her breathing had slowed. 'You're in London.'

Her pie lay untouched on the desk, but she was no longer hungry. Outside the grey sky had finally fulfilled its promise and rain was falling heavily, turning the slope into a running river. She sighed, stood up, and prepared to change once more into her pierrot costume.

The inspector had again warned the cast about not walking home alone, not that they needed reminding, thought Dorinda. There was a slightly febrile edge to the evening's performance. Again, Dorinda scrutinised the audience, damp and now steaming in the heat of the auditorium, carefully, but was unable to identify anyone who looked, to her eyes, like a criminal. The well-dressed gentleman had not reappeared since his first visit, but Dorinda was now aware that anyone, whatever they looked like, could be involved in this wicked trade in human suffering. For she was sure they did suffer, these unfortunate young women – and boys.

The rain was still falling when they saw the audience, still gently steaming, out into the night at the end of the performance. The company gathered in the foyer in their everyday clothes, all the girls looking nervous. Maude helped Dorinda into her grey flannel skirt and white blouse and jammed the small straw hat on top of her hastily constructed bun.

'Come on, then,' said Will. 'Let's go.' He ushered the

company out and turned to lock the doors after Maude and Dorinda.

'At least they haven't got far to go,' said Dorinda, as they watched the rest of the company up the slope. 'Perhaps we should have moved in there, too.'

'As you said before, no room,' said Maude. 'Come on.'

They were halfway up the slope when Dorinda felt a tug on her skirt. She grabbed Will's arm and whirled round in one movement. Behind her, cowering back against the railings was a small and very wet and ragged little boy.

'What -' began Will, but Dorinda hushed him and crouched down to the child's level.

'Did you want me?' she asked gently.

'Please, Miss,' he said, in a hoarse whisper, 'she said as to fetch you.'

'She? Who?' Maude had crouched down beside Dorinda. The boy regarded her from frightened eyes.

'Dunno, Miss.'

'Are you Joe Briggs' boy?' Dorinda asked him.

The child nodded.

'And a lady sent you to fetch me?'

He nodded again. 'Weren't no lady,' he added.

Dorinda straightened up. 'Maude, you go back inside and telephone the police station. Will and I will go with the boy.'

Will and Maude both protested vigorously.

'It's not safe!' said Will. 'Who knows where he'll take us?'

'She said just you, Miss,' said the child, with another tug on Dorinda's skirt.

'How do you know it's me you want?' asked Dorinda.

'She said the lady who talked nice.'

'The lady can't go on her own, lad,' said Will.

'Won't be on 'er own. Be with me.'

It seemed they were at an impasse. Maude solved the problem by turning back and unlocking the doors.

'Come inside,' she said. 'We'll get the boy dry.'

It took all three of them to get the child inside, where he was persuaded to sit down in the foyer between Maude and Dorinda, who indicated with a jerk of her head that Will should go into the office. With a swift nod, he disappeared.

'Now,' said Dorinda, putting an arm round the almost skeletal shoulders. 'Tell us where you've been and all about the person who told you to find me.'

There was an ominous trembling of the bottom lip, and the child ducked his head. Dorinda and Maude exchanged despairing looks.

'Where did you go, luvvie?' asked Maude. 'After the netting shed?'

'Away.'

'On your own?' said Dorinda.

He nodded.

'Why did you go?' Maudie laid a gentle hand on the boy's arm. 'Away from your dad?'

This brought the boy's head up sharply. Then he nodded.

'Ah.' Dorinda began to understand. 'You ran away from your dad? You didn't like the boat?'

A vigorous nod.

'Where'd you go?' asked Maude.

A shrug. 'Dunno.'

'You hid somewhere,' stated Dorinda. 'When did you meet the lady?'

'She were there.' He looked up, first at Dorinda, then at Maude. 'She were tied up.' He was gaining confidence. 'An' this toff come. So I hid.'

'What did he do?' asked Maude.

'Talked. An' then…' he shut his eyes.

'Did he hurt her?' Dorinda said quietly.

Another nod.

'Aramantha?' mouthed Dorinda to Maude. She gave a brisk nod.

'Did you talk to her after that?' she said.

Another nod.

'And that was when she told you to come and find me?'

'She said as you'd 'elp.'

Will came out of the office.

'They said they'll send someone over from Deal. Fred Fowler or his son will be in the town somewhere, but they can't get hold of them.'

'Constable Fowler might come and check on The Alexandria if he sees the light on. Turn up the gas Will,' said Dorinda, 'and now – what's your name?'

'Jim.'

'All right, Jim, now try and explain where this place is? I can't help if I don't know where this lady is.'

He screwed up his face. 'T'other end. Round the top.'

'The top?' Dorinda looked at Will and Maude in puzzlement.

'What the locals call where the lighthouse is,' explained Will. 'I think I know where. There's an old boathouse – I wonder Fred didn't look there for the boy. Or his dad, come to that.'

'Shall we go then?'

'No!' said Maude. 'That toff might come back. Do you think it's the same one who came here?'

'And what does he want?' Dorinda frowned.

A sharp rap on the door took them all by surprise. Jim Briggs shrank into Dorinda's side, as Will went to answer it.

'All right in there?' came Fred Fowler's voice.

Will opened the door a crack. 'I'll come out, Fred.'

'What'll they do?' whispered Maude. 'We've got to get Aramantha somehow.'

Will put his head round the door. 'Fred and me'll go up to the top and see what's what. You stay here with the boy.'

After they'd gone, silence descended. Dorinda felt little Jim Briggs relax against her and realised he was almost asleep. She wondered what would happen to him now – she felt fairly sure his father wouldn't leave this escapade unpunished.

Suddenly, Maude started up.

'What?' whispered Dorinda.

'Shhh!' Maude pointed at the door, which was slowly beginning to open.

CHAPTER SIXTEEN

'Stay where you are.' The well-dressed gentleman – now looking rather dishevelled – slid in through the opening. Jim began to howl. 'And shut that boy up.'

At the sight of the shiny barrel of a small pistol, Dorinda hugged the boy tighter. She felt her heart thudding so loudly she was sure it could be heard by them all.

'What do you want?' Maude said bravely, only a tremor in her voice betraying her fear.

'I want him.' He pointed at Jim. Dorinda tried to muffle his cries against her breast, but it didn't seem to help.

'Why?' she said. This seemed to confuse him.

'I saw those two go away. Where are they going?'

'To fetch more policemen,' said Dorinda bravely.

He laughed – a manic bray. 'Police? Here? Just give me the boy.'

He came towards Dorinda, still pointing the gun. Maude stood up, as if preparing to attack.

'No, Maude!' said Dorinda, and clasped Jim even tighter. 'What do you want him for?'

'Shut up.' He reached forward and grasped her arm, pulling it free from Jim, who immediately darted up and behind Maude.

'Right,' snarled their attacker. 'I'll have to take you, too.'

'Take me where?' gasped Dorinda, as she struggled to free herself.

'Back to the other whore.' He didn't look certain of this, and Dorinda realised he really didn't know what to do with any of them. This was dangerous and could only lead to his losing all control. She stopped struggling and stood up.

'All right,' she said. 'I'll come.'

He gaped at her.

'Come on, then. Or don't you want to, now?'

Without warning she felt a stinging blow on the side of her head. Her vision blurred and pain burst through her as she fell to the floor. Something else was happening. She was being dragged by her arm, and everything hurt. Her arm, held in a merciless grip, her knees, her feet, dragging against the floor.

Now she was aware that she was outside and tried to clear her vision. There was sound, a background mumble that eventually resolved itself into a voice, and then the movement stopped. Her head hit the floor, and everything disappeared again.

Then she was flying. No – someone was holding her and shouting. She was suddenly aware that the shouting was all around her, and she opened her eyes. All she could see was something dark and she felt so sick. Everything faded in and out.

She became aware that there was a change but she couldn't tell what, until a gentle hand was under her arm and the noise that penetrated the pain resolved itself into a child's crying and male voices.

She realised she was sitting back on one of the foyer

chairs, and Maude was sitting on another cradling Jim Briggs on her lap. Next to her, Jack Colyer was peering anxiously into her face and standing in front of the office door, their attacker was being held by Constable Robert Fowler and another uniformed policeman.

'What happened?' she managed to ask.

Colyer let out a hissing breath. 'He damn near killed you, that's what happened. Why did you let him in?'

'We didn't,' Maude cut in. 'And Dorinda ought to be lying down at home, not being questioned by you.'

Colyer looked somewhat shamefaced. 'I know. But we've only got the one motor car, and we must take this – this -' he took a deep breath and indicated the man being held, 'to the police station. I'll go and find you a hackney.'

'At this time of night?' said Maude. 'You'll be lucky!'

'I'll walk,' said Dorinda and attempted to stand up.

'Inspector!' called Robert Fowler. 'This feller 'ere's got a motor car.'

'How do you know?' Colyer turned sharply.

'Left it up the top,' said Robert triumphantly. 'We can take 'im to the station in that. You take the ladies 'ome.'

'Thank you, Constable,' said Colyer, amused, while the other officer protested, red-faced, at his colleague's presumption.

This programme was followed, although Dorinda didn't take much notice. She was dimly aware of Maude explaining what had happened since the appearance of Jim Briggs, whom she had insisted on bringing with them. Once delivered back to their lodgings, Colyer insisted on carrying Dorinda up to the bedroom, under the scandalised eyes of their landlady, before departing to follow Constable Fred and Will.

It wasn't until the morning, after Maude had ushered in a local doctor summoned by the police, that Dorinda began to ask questions.

'I don't know, Dolly,' said Maude, sitting on the edge of the bed. 'Gawd, you gave us a fright. What did the doctor say?'

Dorinda pulled a face. 'I'm supposed to stay here. But I can't – we've been through all this before. I have to play for you.'

Maude exploded. 'We've cancelled, you silly woman! How could we go on with you like this? The others are all going to the station as usual,' -Dorinda suddenly remembered it was Saturday – 'and they'll tell everyone. Stop worrying.'

Dorinda subsided back against her pillows. 'And what about Aramantha?'

Maude looked serious. 'Will said they found her, tied up and filthy dirty – she wouldn't have liked that – and all she could say was that she'd told young Jim to bring you, not the police.'

'What have they done with her?'

'They took her to the police station in Deal, too. Inspector Colyer, when he got there, seemed to think that was the right thing to do.' She shrugged. 'I don't know what to make of it. And that cove last night – what was all that about? Would he have killed us all?'

'I think he was frightened, too, but I don't know why. I think maybe he saw Jim coming to us and wanted to stop him talking – even though Jim didn't know anything. How is Jim, by the way?'

Maude grinned. 'Our Lady Anderson will be along later to tell you. You just be patient. And your Inspector's coming to call, too. He'll tell us what's been going on.'

'Then I must get up. I can't see him here.' Dorinda swung her legs out of bed and was gratified to find that she could stand. 'Give me a hand, Maudie.'

However, it wasn't until almost four o'clock in the afternoon that both Ivy, with a considerably cleaned up Jim Briggs, and Inspector Colyer arrived at the lodgings. Maude busied herself fetching tea, while Jim was allowed to go back to Ivy's chauffeur, Billy, and inspect the inner workings of the motor car. 'Better than fishin'!' he announced.

'Go on, Ivy,' said Maude. 'Tell Dolly and the inspector what you've been doing.'

Ivy, resplendent in her most respectable outfit, grinned smugly. 'Been buying Jim Briggs!'

'What!' gasped Dorinda. '*Bought* him?' Colyer merely raised amused eyebrows.

'He didn't want to go back to his father,' said Maude, 'and he said he liked horses.'

'So, she telephoned me from the theatre. Clever that. And asked if Billy could use a stable lad. And I said he could if I said so.'

Dorinda laughed, until she realised it hurt. 'So – what? You paid off Joe Briggs?'

'He'll only spend it on drink,' said Ivy, 'but there won't be a boy to hit.'

'What about Aramantha and Jim's "toff"?' asked Dorinda asked, when they had all exclaimed about Ivy's generosity.

'It was much as we expected,' said Colyer. 'Ethel Small -'

'Please,' interrupted Dorinda, 'could you start at the beginning? With Jessie and her step-father?'

'It isn't pleasant,' said Colyer.

'I know,' said Dorinda bravely. 'I've learnt a lot in the last few days, and over the last two seasons, as a matter of fact. I won't be shocked.'

Ivy, Maude and Will all looked dubious, but Colyer sighed, leant back in his chair and began.

'Jessie ran away from home before her mother remarried and was making quite a good career for herself when her step-father turned up. At first, he merely tried to intercept her and tell her what she was doing was immoral. She ignored him, but then the other people, particularly women, started coming with him and the banners and chanting started. Finally, he began approaching her and trying to attack her. That really scared her, but at that point, she lost her job at two of her regular halls, which was when she turned to Ada.'

'And then to you, Ivy,' said Dorinda.

'They suggested she come down here, as you know. What neither you nor she knew was that Brother Anarawd and his "followers" had also come down here. He was still pursuing his step-daughter, who for some reason he saw as his property, hoping to take her back to one of the – er – clubs he frequented in town.'

'One of those clubs where Aramantha worked?' put in Maude.

Colyer nodded. 'Unfortunately for him he was recognised, not just by Jessie, but by Aramantha, who decided to try a little blackmail.'

'Blackmail!' said Ivy. 'Blimey!'

'Oh, no.' Dorinda closed her eyes.

'And then he was murdered.' Colyer looked briefly at Dorinda. 'And no, it wasn't Ethel - Aramantha, although she was worried someone would think it was. Foolishly, she sent a telegram to the club.'

'A *telegram*?' gasped Dorinda. 'That was dangerous, surely? Anyone could have read it!'

'Indeed.' Colyer nodded. 'But I imagine she took care to couch it in rather less forthright terms. So, when their representative, who we gather is actually a member of the consortium which owns the premises, and others like it -'

'Jim's toff?' asked Will.

'Jim's toff,' confirmed Colyer, 'appeared, she decided to try the blackmail on him, too. Not about the girls, but about the boys.'

'And he kidnapped her?' said Maude.

'Why didn't he kill her?' asked Dorinda.

'This man, Sebastian Wilcox, knew about Jessie and her act, and it appears there's a taste for it. Male impersonation.' He glanced at Dorinda again.

'So he – what? What did he try to do?'

'As far as we can tell, he was hoping to persuade her to help get Jessie away from you. He kept Aramantha in the boathouse, threatening her and near starving her. Then

132

young Jim appeared, having run away. Unfortunately, when he paid his last visit, he saw Jim leave the boathouse and followed him here. I don't think he was in his right mind from the time he arrived in Nethergate and killed Brother Anarawd. He was scared stiff. He's a very well-respected man in the City – moves in the first circles.'

'So what will happen to Aramantha?' asked Dorinda.

'I don't know,' Colyer admitted. 'I think she'll be charged, but what the offence will be I can't tell yet. She's being as helpful as she can be at the moment.'

Dorinda was frowning. 'What I don't understand,' she said, 'is why Wilcox killed Evans, or Anarawd, and why did he have two names anyway?'

'Evans? Well, as a regular client of the clubs he frequented, he would hardly wish to be known as Brother Anarawd, and as a lay preacher he certainly would not wish to be known as Evans. What is unclear at the moment, and I don't suppose we will ever know, is why the two sides of his character were merged when he married Jessie's mother. As to why Wilcox killed him, he was considered to have become a risk to the people running the illegal clubs. He had more or less revealed himself to Jessie remember, when he attacked her, even though she knew nothing about the clubs, and from what Ethel Small tells us, to her as well. And Ethel was a threat, especially when she showed her hand.'

'Well, I'll tell you one thing,' said Ivy, accepting another cup of tea from Maude, 'I'm not bringing any more girls down here from London. They've made so much trouble for Dolly.'

'And don't anyone talk her into leaving The Alexandria,' said Maude. 'She's been the making of it.'

Dorinda looked round the group and smiled. 'I won't and next year I hope we can turn it into a full-scale theatre and keep going all year, not just the season.'

'So we won't have to go to London!' said Maude.

'So you won't be coming up to town, then?' said Colyer, turning to Dorinda.

'No.' She shook her head.

'Perhaps, then,' he said standing up, 'it's a very good thing that I've been offered the post of Area Superintendent down here in Nethergate.'

DEATH PLAYS A PART
Lesley Cookman

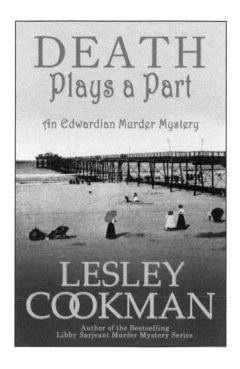

Dorinda Alexander is a former governess who now owns the Alexandria Theatre in the seaside town of Nethergate. Her troupe is rehearsing for a season of music hall performances, a new experience for the theatre – and when mysterious young singer Velda Turner arrives looking for employment Dorinda, impressed by her talent, hires her.

But soon optimism turns to tragedy when a body is found after an apparently motiveless break-in at the theatre.

Proudly published by Accent Press

www.accentpress.co.uk